Reunited By Choice

Cascade Bay, Volume 2

Solara Gordon

Published by THE EARTH MOVED, LLC, 2022.

REUNITED BY CHOICE

First edition. April 2, 2022.

Copyright © 2022 Solara Gordon.

ISBN: 978-1737305996

Written by Solara Gordon.

Also by Solara Gordon

Cascade Bay
Love Reborn
Reunited By Choice

Peyton Corners
Falling for You
Caught by Love's Slow Burn

Standalone
A Heart's Desire
To Love You Again
To Love You Again

Watch for more at https://solaragordon.com/.

This one is for all that have dared to take a second chance at love, a second chance at romance and a second chance at being together. This one is for my readers, my street team and readers group, Solara's Glamourous Stars, my loves past, present and future, and for me. Writing Tim and Susan's story took me through a healing process, allowed my heart and mind to continue saying yes to love, yes to the magic of falling in love again and embracing the love already in my life. Thank you to my beta readers, my Life and Domestic Partner, Jim Fleckenstein and to all the wonderous people who have touched my life with love, passion and the courage to embrace all of life's second chances.

Chapter One

"You did *what*?" Susan Nealson winced at the echo her voice created bouncing off the back wall of the corner booth she sat in. She laid her fork down. A quiet homecoming breakfast with her best friend, Nina Carlson, wasn't happening.

Nina sat across from her sipping her coffee. "I paired you up with Tim. Leslie and I have enough going on with his parents and keeping them civil."

Susan leaned forward and spoke in a lower tone. "Keeping Leslie's parents civil?"

Nina set her mug down, nodding. "Cordial is probably a better term. Neither of them is likely to say something drastic. This wedding is stressful enough."

"I'm sorry I wasn't around to help more." Susan bit into her toast, savoring the cashew butter spread topping it.

"Don't sweat not being around. You're here now. Leslie's sister helped a lot." Nina cut into her medium-rare breakfast steak. "Leslie's stepmom and stepdad are great at keeping things calm."

Susan wiped her mouth and replied, "I bet. In high school, Leslie used to mimic his parents arguing. Said it was the only way he stayed sane."

"They had some humdingers. I remember waking up hearing them yelling at each other like they were in my house, not next door." Nina glanced at her watch. "I've got to be at work soon."

Susan picked up her fork. "Here's to enjoying the rest of our breakfast."

Nina nodded. Several moments passed as they ate in companionable silence.

Susan leaned back against the booth as she finished eating, going back over her decision to move back to Cascade Bay. Opening her party planning business was paying off. She had enough local clients to keep her busy for quite a while. Partnering with Jeff Nickerson and Mary Bates made moving back to

Cascade Bay worth the move. Susan wiped her mouth, reaching for her tea. "I'd forgotten how good Maxon's breakfasts are."

"Since Jeff took over, business has grown. His mom retired a couple months ago." Nina nibbled the last of her toast.

"I'm glad he kept her recipes and added his." Susan ate the rest of her eggs, relishing the rich flavors in each bite. "A world-class chef cooking in a diner and loving it."

Nina smiled. "Yes, Jeff got the best of both worlds. Traveled to learn his skill and do what he loves. Now that he's doing catering, he's going to be in demand."

Susan swallowed her last bite of toast and finished her tea before speaking. "Oh, yes!" she began, leaning forward. "Mary's and my business doubled in the last week. Flowers and food go together. Who knew Cascade Bay held so many parties?"

Nina pulled her wallet out of her purse. "Us since we were kids."

"Smart mouth," Susan teased back. "True. With a lot of people moving to Cascade Bay, we've grown."

"Yes, and folks come to get away from the city. I'm sure you'll see more business as summer progresses."

"Probably. I've got four weddings and a couple of graduation parties booked for the next two months." Susan took her wallet out of her tote bag. "Good thing I blocked the week out."

Nina laughed. "I'll say. Your final dress alteration appointment is at two this afternoon."

"That I'll make. No client meetings until four." Susan reached for the check lying on the table. "I'll take care of this. Business is good."

Nina pulled a five and three singles out of her wallet. She laid them on the table between them. Susan started to push the money away as Nina spoke. "Tip. Zach works extra shifts to make ends meet. He starts grad school in September."

Susan grinned. "Hard to believe he's twenty-five."

"My kid brother. Grown, engaged, and going for his master's." Nina glanced over her shoulder as she slid out of the booth. "I still keep an eye on him."

Susan snickered. "Don't let him hear you. He'll give you that 'I'm grown' lecture again."

Nina turned around, shaking her head. "Oh, he knows. He told me he does the same for me."

"Wow, that's great." Susan slung her tote and purse over her shoulder, making her way between the tables toward the diner's front door.

"Too bad you and your sister couldn't mend things." Nina caught up with her. "She missed out."

"We both did. Mom and Dad's divorce kept us apart for many years." Susan stopped at the cash register near the entrance. "Growing up in different cities didn't help either."

Nina raised her hand, waving. "Hey, Jeff. Great meal."

Susan held up the check. "Thanks. I'll see you and Mary this afternoon. The Murphys are eager to sample your suggestions."

Jeff held up his hand, calling out, "Be there in a moment." Susan looked at Nina and winked.

Jeff Nickerson stood six foot two. The chef's hat added another five inches to his height. Some folks backed away at first look. His hazel eyes lit up when he smiled with a warmth that reached out and embraced everyone.

"Glad you enjoyed the meal. Did Zach include your discount?" Jeff asked, reaching for the check as he reached the cash register.

"Yes. You're not going to make money if you keep discounting things." Susan handed him the check and cash she held.

"Regulars." Jeff nodded toward Nina. "And business partners"—he grinned as his gaze met hers—"get them."

Susan opened her mouth to reply only to be interrupted by Jeff hastily adding, "My business, my decisions. Our business, our decisions."

"True enough. See you at four?" Susan dropped the change Jeff handed her in the tip jar next to the register.

"You bet. I'll pick up Mary. She's got some sample floral arrangements to show the Murphys."

Nina moved to the door. "Thanks again, Jeff, for helping out with the tutoring group last night."

"Any time. Now back to the kitchen." Jeff gave them a bow, grinning as he came back up.

Laughing, Susan pushed on the door, opening it. She waited until she and Nina were outside to pick up their conversation. "So you paired me with Tim. I've got one question."

"Okay. What?" Nina pulled her sunglasses down from on top of her head.

"Why?" Susan fished her clip-ons out of the outer pocket of her tote. She fastened them on her glasses as she faced Nina. Nina's sunglasses hid her eyes. Wisps of her red shoulder-length hair blew in the wind coming in off the ocean. Two of Nina's bridesmaids matched her fair complexion, long hair, and model-like figure. Certainly more like what Tim dated in high school and the Cascade Bay newspaper society photos showed him.

"Does it really matter?" Nina took her car keys out of her purse. "It's not like you don't know each other."

"Yes. Don't tell me you've forgotten how disastrous our attempts at dating turned out?" Susan stepped out from under the awning covering Maxon's entrance. Nina kept pace with her as they started walking toward where they parked their cars.

"I didn't forget. We all made mistakes in high school and college. Besides, it's not like I'm setting you and Tim up." Nina picked up her pace.

Susan let Nina get a few steps ahead of her. Pairing up with one of Leslie's groomsmen wasn't the same as a blind date. She'd met everyone in the wedding party at various times. She'd had enough blind dates go sour on her to make her cautious about getting set up. Still, getting paired up with Tim could turn out like those less-than-stellar blind dates. She waited until they reached the corner before responding.

Nina pushed the walk light button several times vigorously. On her last push, Susan nudged her. "I don't believe you. You're acting like I caught you bullshitting me."

Nina spun around and pulled her sunglasses down her nose, revealing her glare. "You can't leave well enough alone, can you?"

"You set us up, didn't you?" Susan tried to inhale. Her hand fisted, clenching tight against her palm. Tim's icy stare and good-bye retort after their last date clung to her as though it were yesterday instead of seven years ago. The pain had dug so deep into her, she had hidden from the world in her dress and mannerisms for the next two years. Now she was supposed to spend a week walking on eggshells around the man who ripped her heart and soul to shreds. Sweat rolled across her palms, slicking her fingers as the light changed.

Nina trotted across the street. Susan matched her pace, unwilling to let her get away. Nina," Susan called out. "Answer me."

Nina stopped near her car, took off her sunglasses, and faced her. "Leslie and I didn't set you up. Tim asked for you."

Susan blinked. Her eyes widened. She tried to speak, opening and closing her mouth. She managed after several tries to croak out, "*Asked for me?*"

"Yes, *asked*. He said he knew you and that's all he would say when I asked why." Nina put her sunglasses back on and unlocked her car. She tossed her purse inside.

"Nina, I'm sorry—" Susan began.

"Accepted. I need to get to the office." Nina got in her car and slammed the door. Susan heard the click of the door locks. Nina's short, terse tone told of her frustration. Even her posture before she got in her car hinted at her growing agitation. She'd stood with her feet apart like she was weighing every word and ready to lash out. Her reddening cheeks capped it.

Susan reached toward the window, ready to rap on it when the car started. Nina pulled away without even looking at her.

Taking a deep breath, Susan counted as she exhaled, visualizing her angst sloshing off her. Mistakes happened. Each of them needed time and space to cool down. As she walked to her car, one thought preoccupied her—why had Tim asked for her?

Chapter Two

Tim Smith looked up from the spreadsheets strewn across his desk. His best friend and Cascade Bay's mayor, Leslie Snider, sat in front of him. Copies of the same spreadsheets lay before Leslie. Combing his fingers through his short red curls, Tim spoke. "Not really a *'yahoo, we did it'* quarter."

Leslie leaned back in his chair, chuckling. "We came pretty close. A good quarter overall."

Tim nodded. "A nice profit. Business is picking up."

Leslie stretched, leaned forward, and picked up one of the spreadsheets. "Foot traffic along Main Street picked up last month. Two of the shops asked about leasing more space."

"Investing in the city makes sense. You approved the expansion, right?" Tim reached for the pen closest to him, handing it to Leslie to sign off on the spreadsheet.

"Sure did. The arcade and skating rink hired three more teens from the high school's entrepreneurs' club."

Tim grinned. "And Mr. Bowman thought we weren't paying attention in econ class."

"Worked our asses off for every extra credit we could get in economics, and accounting classes helped." Leslie picked up another sheet.

"I still remember the look on Bowman's face when they posted the university scholarship awards list." Tim leaned forward to see what sheet Leslie held. "Cascade Bay Drive development?"

"Yes. Three new businesses going in. Either an apartment or condo building is under consideration. Needs county and city approval." Leslie laid the sheet on top of the others. "Enough numbers. My mind is ready to scream."

"Agreed. How about a beer and a game of pool?" Tim gathered his sheets and put them in the folder on the corner of his desk

Leslie stood, rolling his shoulders. "Sounds good. Except make mine a root beer. Nina and I are meeting her parents for dinner."

"Okay, root beer and bumper pool at my place in an hour." Tim put the folder in the middle drawer of his desk and locked his desk. He walked over to the chair holding his backpack. He slid one strap onto his shoulder and picked up the helmet on the corner table closest to his office door.

"Meet you there." Leslie strode out of the office in front of Tim. He stopped halfway down the hall, turned around and walked back to Tim.

"Forget something?" Tim asked, pushing the elevator button.

"Nina's question for you." Leslie pulled his cell phone out. "To quote her, 'Susan demanded to know why you chose her.'"

Tim glanced up at the elevator floor indicator. One more floor until it reached him. He needed a quick response. As the bell rang and the door opened, he said, "I'll tell you at my place. See you there."

Tim didn't wait for Leslie's reply. If Leslie pressed him for a response, he'd either stammer or blurt out where his thoughts scattered. He wasn't sure admitting what his conscience tossed at him would do. He moved inside the elevator and pressed the door-closed button, blocking out anything else other than an image that captured him.

God, a weekend started more things than just a couple of nights of hot sex. Leave it to his cousin and bride to elope to Vegas. He, Susan, and a handful of his cousin's and the bride's close friends went along to witness the nuptials. His cousin gave him the key to his room since the hotel upgraded their room on the house. What happened in Vegas hadn't stayed there. The weekend remained one of his most cherished memories. The first time he got to show Susan the passionate side of his feelings for her. Tim swallowed hard as the elevator bell rang again. Looking up, he noticed the elevator car had reached the first floor. He glanced around him. No one else occupied the elevator. Great, he stood in the middle of the elevator without realizing it. As he exited, Tim nodded to the receptionist outside the first-floor office. He pushed the large glass door open, pulled on his sunglasses, and stepped outside into the midafternoon heat. The sun beat down heating the air several degrees warmer than predicted. Santa Ana winds whipped around the downtown buildings like toddlers chasing each other through an obstacle course. Dust and debris swirled up over the curb, settling in places where the wind bursts didn't reach. As he came to the corner, Tim unbuttoned the top button of his shirt, loosened his tie, and sighed.

The light changed, and a loud horn sounded, accompanied by sirens. Tim looked both ways and behind him. Two engines with a full accompaniment of lights flashing, sirens wailing, and horns blaring zipped by followed by an ambulance and two police cars. Another accident out on the coast highway no doubt. Height of the summer and folks crowding to get out of town away to someplace sandy had the highway more crowded than usual. Tim shook his head. He didn't get it. He liked living close to the ocean. Beaches were great places to jog, walk, and relax. When the crowds started hitting capacity, he stayed away. His backyard workout pool provided the exercise and lap swimming he liked. Northern California Pacific waters temperatures warmed some in August. Otherwise, that cold water could refreeze an ice cube twice over.

"May those needing help find it," he prayed, walking the two blocks to the city parking garage. His car, a red sportster with a sunroof, sat two parking spaces over from the exit. His days of four-door sedans and carpool activity with a car full of talkative children were behind him. His ex and two teens decided moving half a state south made more sense than staying near dad, their friends or the town where they'd spent most of their life. Tossing the helmet and his backpack in the back seat, Tim grinned. The bright red helmet with racing stripes would stand out. His nephew had asked for top-of-the-line motorcycle racing gear for his birthday.

Tim rolled up his sleeves, took off his tie, and opened the sunroof. The forty-five-minute drive home would give him time to come up with a plausible reason why he'd chosen Susan.

Four traffic lights and two slow left turns brought him to the highway. He turned on the CD player, cranked up the volume, and entered the highway. Speed, music, and very little traffic brought him the focus he needed. Explaining to Leslie or Nina about Susan wasn't going to be easy. He had to come up with something.

"Okay, Tim." He began thinking out loud. No one could hear what he said due to the music volume and the speed he drove. "Susan's got you intrigued. Now, why and how."

Tim shook his head as he worked his thoughts back to their last unencumbered conversation. That was two...no, three... frack! It was seven years ago. Tim smacked the stirring wheel with the palm of his hand. A high-pitched horn sounded. He glanced around. Good, no one close by. Boy, that was dumb! Taking a deep breath, Tim let go a deep pent-up sigh, gripped the stirring wheel, and changed lanes. The sign he passed showed less than a quarter-mile to his exit.

So much for going backward and gathering his thoughts. Susan laughed at his lame jokes. She understood him because they shared history. Even chewed his teen and college self out when he needed it and hugged the stuffing out of him afterward. Then why the hell hadn't their relationship attempts worked out?

Because you always had to be right, a voice screeched in his mind. Tim scowled. His conscience sounded like his ex when she cranked up her whine, refusing to take no for an answer. Great, he wasn't looking for chastisement. He wanted answers, not his child brain acting out.

Maybe there was a point to that thought though. Neither he nor Susan confided in each other beyond close friends. The few times they did were usually on shared experiences. Both of them had lacked best friends throughout high school. He and Leslie ran into each other at college their freshman year, became roommates and best friends. Had Susan and Nina's friendship grown due to similar circumstances? So many questions and so much unknown. As Tim pulled up to a stoplight, he snapped his fingers. He smiled as he turned onto the main drag leading into his housing complex. He had enough to keep Leslie and Nina from pestering him further. At least until he had his thoughts formulated better.

"I chose Susan because I know her." Tim smiled more as he said it again. The unsettled part of their past might keep them on eggshells for now. Given his dreams and sexual fantasies as of late, he wanted another chance. A chance at what he still needed to figure out.

"Seven years, and I still got the hots for her." Tim rolled his eyes heavenward, ready to blow a raspberry at the sky. Sounds of a car downshifting roared through the open sunroof.

He glanced in the rearview mirror. A blonde in a convertible with the top down, her hair blowing in the wind, pulled up behind him. He knew that license plate. It belonged to only one person, Caryn McStone, the daughter of one of Cascade Bay's upper crust families. There was a time when Caryn and women like her got his attention and focus. His ex-wife hung out with that crowd like many of the women he used to be attracted to. One woman held his rapt attention—Susan. He got part of why that was. Putting it into words still baffled him to some extent. The light changed. He eased into the intersection and turned. Getting away from Caryn mattered. He didn't want her tailing him. Some women chased men like a dog after a bone. Word around town was her jet-setting boyfriend dumped her at the airport as they landed. Damn, talk about bad luck. He didn't need hers rubbing off on him. He watched Caryn drive past the street he turned down. She was animatedly talking on her cell as she sped through the intersection. Tim exhaled, muttering a thankful prayer that his good luck continued.

Three blocks from his house, Tim slowed. He watched the houses roll by. Families, some multigenerational ones, owned many of the homes lining both sides of the street. The neatly manicured yards' curb appeal drew gazes as vehicles passed. Three streets over, a four-story building housed the newest addition to this section of town. Condos and the amenities apartment life offered. Many millennials bought the affordable places over the ranch-style homes closer to town. A type of living he didn't care for. Community property laws sometimes worked since he got to keep the investment property he bought before his marriage. Building the place into his post-divorce dream home had worked out to a point. It lacked a few essential ingredients—a wife and children. He found himself thinking about two items a lot since Leslie told him Susan accepted Nina's request to be her maid of honor. Was this a sign he might be getting the second chance he daydreamed about, the one with Susan by his side?

Chapter Three

Tim noted his next-door neighbor's grandkids played on the front lawn with two of their friends. Starting over with babies might not appeal to some thirty-five-year-olds. To him, it did. He wanted a family where the mom and dad raised their children together. Not separate households half a state apart. This time he knew what he wanted, to be a dad again. The first time came by surprise and at a cost, his and Karlene's budding relationship.

He missed his daughters. Their aloofness and flyby visits left him wanting more. Getting away to visit them in San Diego wasn't easy. They spent more time with their friends and cousins during his last visit. And their infrequent calls and e-mails in response to his left him at odds on how to reconnect with them.

Loud barks sounded as he cut the motor. Opening the car door, Tim pushed the button on the garage door remote, closing it. Another beep sounded, disarming the house alarm system. He jingled his keys, setting off more barking. Sassy and her brother Thorn made their presence known. Two grown Staffordshire Terriers waited on the other side of the door. Had they cornered Mama Cat again? Mama didn't take well to being a doggy pillow. Her cohort, Tabby, tolerated doggy sleep piles until Sassy tried to curl him into a tighter ball. Tim smiled, reaching for the doorknob, knowing he could face another mound of shredded paper given the quartets' demeanors lately.

Unlocking the door, he slowly opened it. Sassy's paw greeted him. She tried to work her paw into the small opening, barking and whining when failure happened. Another deeper bark sounded. Thorn was no doubt right behind her. Tim braced himself, took hold of the doorknob with both hands, and pushed the door inward. Sassy, wiggling, her tail wagging like windshield wipers at top speed, lunged toward him. Tim let go of the doorknob, yelling, "Stop, Sassy. Sit. You too, Thorn."

Quiet's sharp arrival, followed by the pleasant sound of silence, told him both dogs heard him. Tim moved up the steps and into the house. He took a deep breath as he weaved between Sassy and Thorn sitting side by side. How long that would last, he didn't know. He wasn't waiting to find out. Getting to the kitchen mattered. If anything like the last mess he'd come home to awaited him, he knew Leslie would be laughing as he watched the cleanup happen.

Two steps, and he stopped. Inhaled, counted, and let go a deep sigh. No matter what they'd done, he knew he was home. Now if he could find a human companion that greeted him with as much enthusiasm...well, wishes sometimes took trial and error to come to fruition. He hoped his error period with Susan was behind him.

Three more steps and he turned, ready for whatever havoc and mess his furry quartet had for him. Setting his backpack on the counter, he glanced toward the living room. In the rocker in the corner near the window, Mama lay curled up. Her calico coat illuminated by the patches of sunlight beaming through the partially closed blinds. On the couch, sprawled out like he owned it, lay Tabby. After spending most of his ten years outdoors, the old male liked his soft life. Tim shrugged. So far, so good. He rounded the counter and...

He tried pressing his lips together. A hand over his mouth didn't work either. Laughter erupted. He shook his head, glancing back toward the mudroom door. Sassy lay near it with Thorn, trying to look like he didn't know what Tim saw. Tim moved into the kitchen more. In the middle of the area, bits of cotton, fabric, and dog bed littered the floor. As he bent down for the piece closest to his feet, Tim laughed harder. Neat hand-stitched letters greeted him. An S and part of an A remained intact on the small corner he picked up. Near it, another corner lay with a T and an H showing. Tim rolled his eyes as he reached the kitchen trash can. Remnants of fabric shredded lay close to the cabinets where he kept the dog and cat treats. He leaned down examining the face of the cabinet door. No scratch marks marred the finish. "Thank you," he said, holding the trash can. "I wish you two could pitch in on this clean-up."

Sassy rolled over, belly up like she tried to distract him. Thorn ducked his head, looking away. Tim chortled as an image flashed through his mind. His ex, Karlene, bug-eyed, lips tightly pressed together, and her hand on her hips, glaring at him and the dogs. She insisted on the overpriced dog beds and hand-stitching their names on them herself. He tried to warn her. She didn't listen. Nor had his daughters either with the dog toys and squawkers. Sassy could tear a squawker out of a toy faster than a mouse could get away from Mama. Thorn chewed his out within days of getting a new toy. Ah, fur kids—almost as ornery as human ones. Sassy turned over and crawled over to him, laying her head on his feet. "Not now, Sassy. Leslie is on his way." Tim stepped back. Sassy sat up, her tail wagging. Thorn barked. They considered Leslie part of the pack. Tim snorted as he continued stuffing bits and pieces of the destroyed dog beds into the trash. No telling what had set the dogs off. As he turned back to where the trash can went, he saw why the dogs went off. A lavender envelope. Not just any lavender envelope. The exact shade Karlene used. His name stood out in her handwriting. Damn it, he needed to figure out where to hide his spare key better. He thought he'd outfoxed her the last time she found it and used it to get in. He'd contact his lawyer about filing the restraining order as much as he preferred not to. Why was Karlene in town?

He put the trash can down and reached for the envelope as a hard knock sounded at the front door. Two more fast raps followed. Leslie's distinct knock. "Hang on, Leslie," Tim called out, making his way through the hall toward the front door. Sassy and Thorn trailed him barking. As Tim unlocked the door, he moved behind it. Otherwise, he and Leslie would be stumbling off the porch, trying to keep upright as Sassy and Thorn eagerly greeted Leslie.

"Hey," Leslie began as he stepped in. "Sassy, sit, now." She did immediately.

"Why does she listen to you more quickly?" Tim stuck his head around the door.

Leslie shrugged. "Voice? Pitch? Maybe I got the dad voice down."

Tim pointed at Leslie. "You don't have kids."

"No, I got pairs of rambunctious nieces and nephews. My siblings made sure I had training. Remember I babysat them as toddlers." Leslie made his way down the hall toward the kitchen.

"*We* babysat them as I remember." Tim closed the front door and followed Leslie down the hall. "How come I didn't get that training?"

Leslie snickered. "'Cuz you weren't around mocking Amy. She got tired of me doing it. So she challenged me to use it on the kids."

"And it worked." Tim leaned against the counter. "Is that how you ended up in her good graces?"

"That and telling my three other sisters they were going to pay me. They'd run out of other sitters." Leslie faced him. He took off his tie and tossed it on the counter. Rolling his shoulders, he continued. "Nina must be PMSing."

"Oh?" Tim opened the refrigerator, pulling out two cans of root beer. He handed one to Leslie.

"Yes," Leslie sighed, popping the can open. "She's insistent you tell me why Susan."

"Judas Priest," Tim exclaimed. "You'd think I won the lottery and won't share."

Leslie lowered his can, grinning. "Good pun, bro. You gotta come up with something."

"Why?" Tim swallowed part of his soda. He started toward the basement door. "My choice. My decision."

"Things, yeah. People, they got to know." Leslie started to follow him. "Got munchies? Nina is taking Susan for her dress fitting."

"Dinner delayed?" Tim turned around and walked to a cabinet next to the refrigerator. He opened the cabinet. "What you want?"

"Crackers and cheese, potato chips, and another root beer." Leslie opened the cabinet next to the sink, pulling out small bowls.

"Sounds like a snack rather than a few munchies." Tim handed the chip bag to Leslie. "Cracker and cheese packs are all I got for now. Grocery run after we're done."

Leslie picked up the envelope lying on the counter close to where he sat the bowls. "Karlene?" he asked, holding the envelope and turning toward Tim.

"Yes." Tim took the envelope. "She wants or needs something. I gotta hide my spare key better."

Tim tore one corner of the envelope, worked his finger inside, opening the envelope. He pulled out a folded sheet of stationery. He looked up at Leslie, who leaned on the counter watching him. "This can wait."

"No, you need to know what she wants. She's skirting legal action this time." Leslie opened his pack of crackers and cheese and popped one into his mouth. He opened the bag of chips, filling each bowl halfway.

"Yeah, I gotta get a restraining order." Tim shook his head and unfolded the stationery. He looked down and read the short note twice before he looked up.

"Well?" Leslie picked up his root beer. "I haven't seen that look for a while."

Tim inhaled and replied, "Karlene's great uncle left me some money. Also, the girls. She's in town to get his estate taken care of."

"Doesn't sound too bad." Leslie drank from the can he held.

"Not really. She also noted that my neighbor let her in. Mrs. McGee takes care of the animals when I'm out of town." Tim laid the envelope and stationery on the counter. "I'm ready to shoot some pool. Are you?"

"Got my root beer and munchies. Let's shoot some pool." Leslie made his way toward the basement door. Tim followed carrying his munchies.

At the bottom of the basement steps, off to the right, sat a medium-size bumper pool table. Leslie pulled out one of the built-in snack trays. "Your granddad was ahead of his time coming up with these built-ins."

"He and Dad did this years later. They spent many a holiday down here keeping the kids entertained while the cooking went on." Tim sat his snacks on his side. He took a cue stick off the rack, chalked the end, and faced Leslie. "Fast game or play at whatever speed?"

"In between." Leslie selected a cue stick and took the first shot. "Remember, Nina has the meter running on me being there for the parents' dinner."

"I wish you luck. Her parents are corkers." Tim took the next shot. Two balls bounced off the bumpers in the middle of the table, knocking into each other again. They stopped close to the corner pocket near Leslie.

"Our parents can be, too." Leslie slowly pulled his arm back, lining up the shot. "Corner pocket three balls and I call next topic."

"You're on." Tim leaned on his stick, grinning. Leslie's record-making this shot wasn't high. For additional luck, as if it really worked, Tim crossed his fingers. Not that changing the topic mattered.

Leslie drew his arm back and slowly moved it forward. The tip of his cue struck the single-colored ball high on its side, sending it rolling with a leisure momentum toward the eight ball nestled tight to the six ball. Tim rounded the table, ready to line up his shot, when a crack sounded. The balls slipped one after the other into the pocket. Leslie stood up, wet a finger, and dragged it downward. "Score."

Tim bumped his fist against Leslie's. "I bet the topic is Susan."

"You're right. Give me something I can tell Nina." Leslie racked the balls center of the table. He bit into a chip, chewed, and spoke. "Gets Susan off Nina's back, too."

Tim licked his bottom lip, rubbed both lips together, and exhaled. "Easy answer is I know her. She's familiar to me."

"You know Dottie and Beth, too." Leslie popped a cracker and cheese into his mouth.

Tim shrugged as he drank more of his root beer. "Attraction counts, too."

"Explain, please." Leslie took the first shot of the new game.

"Is this twenty questions?" Tim ate more chips, took his shot, and opened his other soda can.

"No, just enough to get the women off my back." Leslie pointed to the table. "Your shot."

"The other two didn't click. They're pretty. There wasn't more than momentary eye candy." Tim took his shot. Three balls, including the eight ball, rolled across the table, hitting the bumpers and shooting into the table pockets near them.

"You're game. I get you on Beth and Dottie." Leslie put his cue stick back in the rack on the wall. He popped another cracker and cheese in his mouth, chewed, and swallowed. "Let's go back upstairs and discuss how I'm going to say this."

"Oh, great. I'm writing speeches for you again!" Tim put his cue stick away. He put his empty cans in the bowl along with the wrapper from his cheese and crackers.

"No, you're dictating the content. I'm writing." Leslie started toward the stairs, carrying his bowl and trash. "The messenger is getting this right."

Tim groaned as he started up the stairs behind Leslie. Telling a woman you didn't click with her took more words than a couple of sentences. What the hell did Leslie have in mind?

"Nina's with Susan at her dress fitting. I'm sure we can come up with enough to appease them both." Leslie placed his bowl in the sink, reaching for the lined pad Tim kept on the refrigerator.

Chapter Four

"Thanks for picking me up," Susan said, fastening her seatbelt after getting into Nina's car.

"You're welcome." Nina pulled away from the curb without looking at her. Susan flinched at the coolness in Nina's voice.

Six hours later and Nina was still miffed. Great. She probably felt she had an apology owed her. Susan felt Nina owed her one. At this rate, neither of them would get one if they kept evading the issue. Susan turned in her seat. Nina looked ahead, avoiding her. Normally, they let things cool some. Then one or the other reached out to discuss what set of the quarrel. Between clients stopping by and deliveries among phone calls, Susan focused on the moment. Business needed her full attention. It wasn't until her phone buzzed that her thoughts moved off the mess that a delayed order created. The alarm reminding her about the fitting appointment came at the right time. She had forty minutes to change gears mentally and grab a quick snack. Susan could feel the hesitation squeeze through with each look they sent each other. Tension thickly filled the air. Silence wasn't going to help. She turned so she faced Nina as best she could.

"I think I owe you an apology." Susan paused, wanting to be sure her next words explained why she reacted the way she had.

"Thanks," Nina replied and kept looking ahead even though they were at a stoplight.

Susan inhaled, let go a deep breath, and continued where she left off. "My experience with blind dates and setups isn't good. Tim is one of those that messed up royally."

Nina glanced at her. She nodded and frowned. Now what? Susan opened her mouth to reply when Nina shook her head. The light changed as she spoke.

"You, Leslie, Tim, and I go way back. When Leslie said Tim was his best man choice, I'd already said you were my maid of honor choice. Beth and Dottie are good friends. Not close and tenured like you and me."

"Okay. I get that. Why pair Tim and me up otherwise?" Susan straightened up in her seat.

"Beth and Dottie's husbands are sitting with them at the reception. You and Tim are the only singles in the wedding party."

Susan pressed her lips together. Times like this being single sucked. She could count the number of men she felt close to one hand. Tim ranked among them, bad history aside. His presence counted for a lot of the weird stuff in her past. Not in a bad way sometimes. "I'm sorry—"

Nina held up her hand, interrupting her. "I'm sorry, too. I knew you would think Leslie and I were setting you up. I told him so."

Susan grinned. "Leslie probably said go ahead, knowing his sense of humor."

"I'm sorry I didn't explain better." Nina reached toward her, her palm up. "We're best friends."

Susan took hold of Nina's hand and squeezed. "We're like sisters. Both of us are stressed by stuff. Apology accepted."

"Yours, too." Nina glanced at her, smiling. "You're gonna love your dress. It's a deep sapphire blue."

"Ooh, my favorite color." Susan beamed. "What about Dottie and Beth's?"

"Their dresses are a similar shade. Slightly different cut." Nina turned into the parking lot of Wedding and Formal Wear, Inc. and parked. "In the outer pocket of my purse, there's a picture of their dress."

"I'll wait until I've seen mine, okay?" Susan got out of the car.

"Sure. The seamstress, Olivia, is familiar with the material and the cut of the dress. She's altered similar dresses before." Nina held open the front door.

"Good. That should help speed things up?" Susan entered, shading her eyes as she walked into the fluorescent-lighted store.

"I hope so. The wedding's two weeks off." Nina pointed toward the counter in the back of the store off to one corner. "That's your dress hanging on the coat rack."

Susan quickly made her way to the back of the store. She stopped in front of the coat rack gazing at the dress. She held out her hand behind her. "Picture, please."

Nina placed the photo in her hand. Susan held the photo up at eye level while glancing at her dress from time to time. The similar color and cut created a subtle difference that worked well together. "The color of my dress is a shade deeper than the others. I'm glad you decided to go with tea-length dresses."

"Thank you. I wanted a dress I could wear again. I went with the same idea for my attendants," Nina said.

"I better try this on so Olivia can start." Susan draped the dress over her arm and walked into one of the corner dressing rooms. She hung the dress up on the hook close to the three full-length mirrors taking up one corner of the small dressing area. She turned to pull the curtain closed. Nina stood close by. She watched as though her thoughts were elsewhere. Susan pulled the curtain closed wondering if this had to do with their conversation en route to the fitting. She let her thoughts drift back to their conversation as she undressed and put the dress on.

A cough sounded, followed by someone clearing their throat. Susan blinked twice, bringing her reflection into focus. The scoop neck bodice framed her bust without over-emphasizing it. The two-inch thick waistband's decorative stitching reminded her of a midnight star-filled sky. Flecks of gold interlaced with silver stitches created the ornamental emphasis that drew her gaze away from the lowness of the neckline. Along the neckline edge, matching stitching etched a lace effect. The short cap sleeves covered enough of her shoulder and upper arm that she didn't feel exposed. Her size sixteen figure might have looked out of place among Nina, Beth, and Dottie. Nina's size-ten figure suited her five-foot-eight height and build. Beth and Dottie wore smaller sizes that required special ordering. Susan slipped out of her sandals and into the kitten heels she brought with her. The black patent leather shoes didn't feel as awkward as other heels did. These were comfortable. She moved to the curtain, pulling it back and stepping into the alteration area.

"Oh my goodness," Nina said. "I chose the cut of the dress based on the prom dresses we wore."

Susan tittered. "That was long ago. I didn't think of that when I put the dress on."

"Then this is a first time for you. What are you thinking?" Nina held two other dresses draped over her arm.

"The cut is great. I don't feel exposed. Like at Lily's wedding when we both pinned part of the V neck closed." Susan moved to the two-step platform center of the alteration room. She watched herself in the full-length mirror across the room as she stepped upon it. Even with her hair pulled back in a simple ponytail, the woman staring back at her didn't fit the one her mind projected of her. The woman in the mirror stood tall. Her shoulders were back without a stark rigidness to them. Her arms spoke of hours working out, gardening, and other strength-related tasks. Her legs showed shape and muscles. Even her smiling face invited people to come up to her and converse. Yes, a very different woman greeted her. One that she knew would dominate her inner thoughts and visions going forward. Clothes could create an altered vision. A change that she possibly resisted. Maybe, just maybe what Tim said all those years ago was right.

"Ma'am, the dress fits you lovely." Olivia reached for the hem. A pincushion wristband stood out on her left arm. Multicolored pinheads decorated the pink-and-purple polka-dotted pincushion.

"Are those for me, too?" Susan pointed at the dresses draped over Nina's arm.

"No, these are Dottie and Beth's." Nina held up one of the dresses. "I wanted you to see them. Beth and Dottie are picking up their dresses today."

Susan turned her head to keep her reflection in view to see the dress Nina held up compared to hers. "The accent embroidery is very similar. Dress color shades complement each other."

"Yes, they do. Sapphire comes in a variety of hues. This shade complements Beth and Dottie very well." Nina hung both dresses on a rack near the dressing room.

"As yours does you, ma'am," Olivia offered, straightening up. "A couple inches off the hem will place the dress at knee length for you. Take a look." Olivia pointed to the mirror.

"Wow," Susan gasped. "That does make a difference." The dress now accented her legs, giving them enough more length to add to her stature without a lot of effort.

Nina coughed. Olivia turned to her. Susan put her hands on her hips, stuck out her tongue, and gave Nina a raspberry cheer. "What now?"

"You and clothes." Nina moved into the dressing room. She turned around holding up Susan's top. "T-shirts and jeans are all you've worn for years."

Susan reached for the faded T-shirt. Nina held it up, out of her reach. "I'm not dressing up to clean the condo."

"You couldn't change before going to your office?" Nina tossed the T-shirt back on the chair inside the dressing room.

"You called as I was on my way to the grocery store."

"You don't care what your clients think?" Nina sat down on the chair closest to her.

"Right now, no. Earlier today, not while I unpacked boxes and cleaned the condo." Susan stepped off the fitting platform.

"And while we ate breakfast?" Nina folded her arms against her.

"Even then. Why? Because I'm not on duty twenty-four-seven." Susan stopped at the dressing room entrance. "I've got a change of clothes with me for my four o'clock appointment."

"All right. What are you wearing?" Nina leaned forward, reaching for her purse she had sat on the floor earlier. She rose, slinging her purse over her shoulder.

Susan turned, faced Nina, and spoke. "What am I wearing? Clothes!" She backed into the dressing room, yanking the curtain closed.

"That isn't an answer. I want to—"

"Ms. Nina," Olivia began.

"Yes."

"Come to the front with me, please. I want to show you some ribbon that might work for the hem of the dress." Footsteps sounded, fading as they got farther away from the dressing room.

Susan let go a deep sigh. She carefully took off the dress, placing it on the hanger. Opening her tote bag, she pulled out the white tank top and slipped it on. Next, she put on a khaki-colored skirt with a two-inch slit in the back. She tucked the tank top in before she threaded a gold chain belt through the skirt's belt loops that clasped in the front, leaving a bit dangling with a gold-colored crystal on the end. A short-sleeved peach-colored shrug came next. Her folded jeans and T-shirt filled the bag. Susan slipped her sandals back on. Nina hadn't noticed the tan strappy sandals lying on the floor near the chair in the dressing room. Susan reached into the interior pocket of her tote. She took out a small pouch, opened it, and took out earrings, a necklace, and a matching bracelet. Finally, she ran a brush through her hair after she took down her ponytail. She quickly braided her hair, looping her hairband around the end of her braid. A few touches of makeup and her business persona came into view. She pulled back the curtain, ready to see what Nina had to say now.

Neither Nina nor Olivia was in sight as Susan exited the dressing room. She stepped out into the walkway leading to the front of the store. She gripped her tote and purse in one hand, ready to battle with Nina. Susan stopped, took a deep breath, and repeated the one mantra she repeatedly used when stress threatened to break her inner peace. "I'm thriving, in charge, and at peace with me."

Olivia turned first toward her. "Ma'am, I didn't see you come in. How can I help you?"

Nina turned as Susan spoke. "Do I look that different?"

Nina's mouth hung open. Susan pressed her lips together, working hard to resist the urge to rock back on her heels, bouncing with delight. One thought followed, calming her as she walked up next to Nina. When people didn't see each other for periods of time, people did and could change.

Chapter Five

Susan looked at her watch as she locked her car door. After Nina dropped her off, she ran a couple of errands, knowing that her meeting with the Murphys might take longer than the hour they agreed upon. Short of the perishables she needed to complete the dinner she anticipated making, the rest of the ingredients sat in the back of her car. Fifteen minutes late wasn't too bad. She picked up her pace as she scanned the other vehicles in the community center's parking lot.

She spotted Jeff's dark gray SUV parked close to the community center's entrance. The center's combination fellowship hall and dining area offered the space needed to accommodate the Murphys' three hundred plus guests and wedding party. The kitchen rivaled any of the local three-star restaurants in town. Jeff knew the appliances from his weekly volunteer duties helping with senior lunches and delivering food to the homeless shelter in San Jose. Thank goodness, Nina and Leslie's guest list was much smaller.

As Susan approached the SUV, she noticed Mary sitting inside, holding her cell phone to her ear. She waved as Susan walked up to the passenger door. Mary rolled down the window, held up one finger, and continued speaking. "That's right, Fifteen hundred red-and-pink carnations, four hundred deep red roses, sixty blue baby roses, and a hundred white-and-lavender tulips."

Mary covered the mouthpiece on her phone. "Hey, Susan. The Murphys decided they want the shop to do the flowers for the wedding and reception. I'll be in in a moment. I've got to get the order in so Greg can go into San Francisco to the flower mart tomorrow."

"That's great. They put a deposit on this, right?" Susan winked as she finished speaking. Mary's business acumen made her the perfect partner. Her magna cum laude degree in accounting from San Jose State combined with her CPA state certification left no doubt who handled the bookkeeping.

"Yes, last week. They handed me their list of colors and final number of wedding party attendants as they arrived." Mary uncovered the phone. "That's right, Greg. We need the small crystal vases, too. I'll get back to you after the meeting. Thanks."

Mary opened her door. "Greg said he would check on prices and then call me back. So let's go rescue Jeff. He's probably out of small talk by now."

Susan walked alongside Mary as they covered the short distance to the community center's entrance. "I'm sure he's doing fine."

Mary smiled as she reached for the door. "Mr. Murphy was talking about his stint overseas while in the army."

"Travel Jeff can relate to and discuss." Susan followed Mary inside.

"Yes, and I heard food mentioned. I doubt he's cowering under a table." Mary grinned as she turned into the hall leading to the fellowship hall.

"Either way, let's get the meeting started." Susan moved in front of Mary making her way toward the open double doors. Jeff's laugh and voice could be heard as he talked with another male. Probably Mr. Murphy, the father of the bride.

"Good afternoon, everyone," Susan called out, entering the room. "Sorry I'm a bit late. Shall we get started?"

She moved to the table set up close to the front of the room. On it sat two four-inch-thick three-ring binders. They housed photos and samples for menus. Next to them sat several covered dishes. Good, Jeff had samples with him.

Jeff walked to the table, opened one of the binders, and pulled out a sample menu printed on thick card stock. He handed them to Mr. and Mrs. Murphy, their daughter, future son-in-law, and his parents. "This is an idea of what you might serve depending on your guests' food preferences, allergies, and tastes."

"Jeff, these menus look good," Cathy Murphy said, laying the sheet she held aside. She pointed to platters of food sitting on the table in front of her and her fiancé, Nick Tang. "Quite a few samples, too."

"Yes, ma'am. Choice often helps with a large number of guests. Two appetizers, two entrées, a vegetarian or vegan option." Jeff moved next to Mary who sat at the end of the table holding the samples. He spoke again. "A pleasing table creates an inviting atmosphere for your guests."

Jeff laid his hand on Mary's shoulder, squeezing slightly. Mary reached up, covering his hand with hers. Susan noted the quick glance they gave each other before looking away. Jeff spoke as he moved to where several bouquets of flowers lay on the opposite end of the table. Next to the bouquets, several centerpiece-size vases sat with varying flower arrangements in them. "Mary handles the floral arrangements and reception decorations. I understand you'll be working with her for the ceremony flowers, too."

"I dropped by the shop after seeing what she'd done for a coworker's vow renewal ceremony." Cathy pointed to the vase holding daffodils and hot pink tulips with sprigs of baby's breath intertwined with them against two large green leaves. "Vibrant colors. I love tulips."

"I spoke with my assistant, Greg. He's got the order to see what the overall cost will entail. I think we'll be okay since the wedding is late October." Mary laid her open planner on the table. She glanced to Susan, who looked up from the pad she scribbled notes on.

"Thank you for choosing us since your original planner canceled out." Susan rose, moving behind the long table. "The church agreed to honor the date. The community center is behind the reception. We're blessed that all the original contracts and reservations got honored."

"Trisha Jenks highly recommended you, Ms. Nealson. I'm glad you're on board." Nick Tang leaned forward. "I'm ready to taste some of these samples."

Cathy nudged Nick. "You and your stomach." She laughed and looked at Susan. "I'm sorry Trisha broke her ankle. I hope everything turns out all right."

"I spoke with her yesterday. She's home and doing well. She asked me to thank you for your understanding and the get-well flowers," Susan replied.

Jeff rose and moved behind the table. "Susan, if you'll help me with this, please."

"Sure," Susan said, making her way around the table. "Mary is passing out utensils and napkins."

"The first dish is a mixed greens salad with arugula, endive, spinach, and kale garnished with chopped egg and bacon. Cheese can be added. The dressing is a raspberry vinaigrette sweetened with a touch of honey. Other dressings can be used." Jeff placed a snack-size portion on each of the paper plates. Mary helped Susan serve them.

"There's a tang with a hint of sweetness. I like that touch. Could you add other items to this?" Cathy's mother asked in between bites.

"Yes, more greens or garnish are doable. Other dressings could be offered." Jeff made notes on the pad in front of him as others voiced their thoughts and impressions.

Cathy looked at Nick. He smiled and nodded before forking his last bite into his mouth. "I think we'll go with the salad with the bacon on the side and more garnishes available."

Nick said, "Several of my family are vegetarian. This will help with their meal choices."

"I'll get back to you with a list of what we can include. I've got a vegetarian entrée to show you, too." Jeff uncovered the next platter. "This is another appetizer that many of your guests may like. Taquitos and spring rolls."

"There is guacamole and sweet-and-sour sauce." Susan sat small cups of each next to the tasters. Mary gathered the used plates while Jeff laid new ones with the taquitos and spring rolls on them in their place.

"The spring rolls can include shrimp or ground beef. These are vegetable. The taquitos are bean. For the vegans attending, the taquitos are plant-based protein."

"These are wonderful," Nick offered, in between bites of each. "I think we've got the appetizers nailed with these. What do you think, Cathy?"

"Agreed. Salad. Taquitos. These spring rolls are yummy." Cathy wiped her hands. "I'm eager to see what you've got for the main course."

"I'd like to suggest something," Nick's mother proposed.

"Yes, ma'am," Jeff said, turning to the woman at one end of the table.

"Tofu might also work for the vegan and vegetarian recipes. I use it." She smiled as Jeff nodded, making notes on the paper again.

"Good choice provided no one is allergic." He looked up at Cathy and Nick. "Might want to check on that with your guests."

Discussions continued as Nick and Cathy finished their samples. Jeff stacked the empty platters together before moving down the table. "For the main entrée, I'm thinking of a choice of fish or beef. In this pan, I've got Swai and Tilapia braised in a white wine sauce with shallots and wilted spinach garnishes." Jeff ladled out two bite-size samples into the bowls in front of him. "To get the full taste, I'm including chunks of each fish with a good dose of the sauce."

Murmurs and nods came from each at the table. Cathy and Nick each gave him a thumbs-up. Jeff smiled and moved to the last platter on the table. "This is beef tips with a béarnaise-and-mushroom sauce. Due to possible allergies and taste preferences, the sauce will be served separately."

Another chorus of approvals rose from the tasters. Nick and Cathy spoke quietly among themselves. Each then turned to their parents. Moments passed as Mary and Susan assisted Jeff packing the platters and clearing the used napkins and utensils from the tables.

"Jeff, I'll get back to you later this week with our choices. I like the idea of a vegetarian entrée, too. What you got?" Nick rose, leaned forward, offering Jeff his hand.

Jeff gripped Nick's hand, shaking it as he responded. "Soy protein loaf. Mashed black and kidney beans mixed with vegan cheese and tofu. Or black bean patties casserole topped with a tomatillo sauce or salsa."

"Sounds delicious," Cathy said, standing as well. She looked at her watch. "Mary showed us around the community center while we waited for Susan to arrive."

Nick helped his mother stand. His father met Jeff as he came back around the table. "Very good food, sir. I approve of my son's choice." He gave Jeff a slight bow. Jeff responded in kind, extending his hand as he rose. Nick's father grinned, taking Jeff's hand, shaking it heartily.

Susan pulled out her planner, motioning Cathy and Nick to her. "I'd like to meet with you in four weeks to go over billing and deposits."

"Next week is good for both of us," Cathy countered, pointing to her and Nick.

"I'm booked the next couple of weeks. Attending a wedding myself." Susan picked up her pen, ready to turn the pages in her planner to the date she had in mind.

"Your own?" Cathy asked, entwining her hand with Nick's.

"My best friend's," Susan replied. She continued looking at her planner. "Does Thursday the fifteenth work for you?"

"I'll have to get back to you." Cathy glanced at her watch again. "We're due at the bakery for cake tasting to make our final decision."

Nick offered his hand to Jeff again. "Sir, I'm looking forward to your meal at our reception. I'll be in contact with you concerning the vegan and vegetarian items."

More parting remarks passed as the group, including Mary, Jeff, and Susan, made their way out of the community center. Jeff stopped near Susan's car. Mary was at Jeff's putting the vases away. Jeff turned to Susan. "Thank you for being late."

Susan faced him. "What do you mean?"

"Mary agreed to another date. We'd been so busy with our own jobs, we hadn't talked." Jeff smiled as he sat down the case he carried. "Neither of us thought to pick up the phone."

Susan laughed. "You've got each other's numbers."

"True. You'd think common sense would take over." Jeff glanced over his shoulder as a car door slammed shut. "Truth is I think both of us were blown away by our connection."

"That can happen. I hope you and Mary continue connecting." Susan unlocked her car door and opened it.

"Me, too." Jeff winked and grinned

Susan grinned, shaking her head. "Okay, I've got to run. I've got a date with a soup pot and some cooking of my own to do. Have a great evening."

"I'll call you," Mary called out as Susan got into her car. She closed the door as Jeff faced Mary, asking her something. Apparently, their first two dates went well. Making out already indicated a spark had gotten ignited. Where it went next was up to them.

Chapter Six

Leslie tossed the pad and pen he grabbed off Tim's refrigerator onto the kitchen table. He pulled out the chair on the opposite side of the table, keeping Tim in view.

"Come on, you know why you chose Susan," Leslie chided Tim as he sat down. Tim placed his bowl in the sink, tossed his empty soda cans in the recycle bin, and pulled out a chair across from Leslie.

"Part of it is I know her. Familiar face and person. I'm not lying." Tim dropped into the chair, reaching for a handful of cashew nuts from the dish in front of Leslie. "If I tell you more, this is between us."

Leslie looked up from where he doodled on the pad. "Okay. What's up?"

"Fantasies." Tim sighed. He laid the hand full of nuts on the table, picking one up as he continued. "Some of them are glimpses from the past. Memories rekindled."

"Fantasies?" Leslie wrote the word on the pad. "More?"

Tim popped two cashew halves in his mouth and chewed. As he swallowed, he nodded. "A whole lot more. I could use another soda. You?"

"Sure. Keep talking as you get them." Leslie picked up the nut dish, dumping a few on the table in front of him.

Tim rose, walking back to the refrigerator as he spoke. "I've felt for years I've owed her an apology. God, at times I was such a dumb ass."

As he came back to the table with two more sodas, Leslie looked up from the pad. "How the hell are fantasies tied in with an apology?"

Tim smirked as he handed Leslie a soda. "Well, one sorta ignited the other."

Leslie opened his mouth. Tim quickly held up a hand as he sat back down. "As I started thinking about whom I'd take to the wedding, Karlene and Susan came to mind. We know I wasn't asking Karlene."

Leslie set the soda can down and rapidly covered his mouth, muffling a cough as he grabbed a napkin from the holder on the table. "Damn, dude, stop with the puns and innuendo."

"None done. I'm serious here. You didn't know I'm not seeing anyone?" Tim popped open his soda and drank.

"All right. Susan is familiar. You want to apologize. Nina is going to do twenty questions on that piece of info." Leslie ate two more nuts. "Didn't know about you being womanless."

"Womanless isn't an issue. No relationship is." Tim slumped back in his chair.

Leslie pointed at Tim. "Why didn't you say so? When did this happen?"

Tim blinked, sighed, and shrugged. "It's not like a guy wants to announce, 'hey, I ain't got a relationship going.'"

"True, but how long?"

"About a..." Tim hesitated, pressed his lips together, and nodded. He looked down as he replied, "A year."

"Wow," Leslie whispered, tossing the pen on the table. He gripped the table and rocked back, staring at Tim. "Breakup must have hit you hard."

"Not as hard as the woman would've liked. It was long distance. Still, my heart came out of it crushed enough that I've been relationship shy. Not this shy since my divorce ten years ago."

"Yeah, it took you a good two to three years to start dating after that." Leslie laid his hands on the table. "So why Susan and now?"

"I saw her a few months back at the park playing with her godchildren. I sat at a picnic table, eating lunch. I was far enough away that she didn't see me."

"This is about kids. Right?" Leslie asked.

"Gut punched me that day. I'd gotten the 'thanks, Dad, but we don't want to spend the summer with you' call from Jennifer and Hailey. I want a family." Tim sat up, drinking more of his soda.

"Susan is comfortable, available, and—you ready to say?"

"Fucking hot." Tim buried his face in his hands.

"The weekend you were in Vegas?"

"Oh yeah. Two days of unadulterated sex. We didn't leave the room until I got the call my shuttle was waiting. Susan was in the shower. I bolted without a good-bye."

"Damn, dude. And you were so cold to her at Angela's wedding the last time you saw her."

Tim looked up. He shook his head as he spoke. "Dumb ass again. Now, do you get why I'm sure why I'm challenged on this? Even though it was seven years ago, I remember the incident like it was yesterday."

"Why didn't you call her? Invite her out to lunch?" Leslie picked the pen up, ready to write again.

"Do you think she'd talk to me after the way I've acted in the past?" Tim picked up the last of the nuts in front of him. He palmed them as if he weighed his next words. He looked up. Tim cleared his throat and spoke. "I realized another thing in the last two weeks. I'm in love with Susan."

Leslie stopped writing, laid the pen on the table, and said, "Dude, you got it hard. I'm gonna tell Nina you chose Susan because of your earlier reasons and you want to talk to her about the past. You want to apologize."

"Sounds good. I hope she doesn't press for more." Tim rose as Leslie tore the sheets off the pad. He reached for Leslie's empty soda can.

Leslie leaned forward and touched his arm. "I'm going to tell Nina that Susan doesn't need to know about the apology. That's between you and Susan. For now, all Nina needs to tell Susan is she's a familiar someone to talk with in between toasts and dances."

Tim laughed as Leslie stood. "Susan is a good dancer. If we stay off our miserable past together, we'll see if we can keep a skirmish from happening."

Leslie reached for the doorknob. He glanced at the clock on the wall. "Crap! I gotta run. I've got forty-five minutes to get across town. I'll call you tomorrow."

Tim walked Leslie to his car. Sassy and Thorn stood beside him, unusually quiet. It was like they'd picked up on the yin versus yang his heart and consciousness were going through. Leslie pulled out, waving as he turned onto the road. Tim walked back into the garage, Sassy and Thorn at his side. One thing he knew for sure—he wasn't going to mess up this chance with Susan. They were together again. He was going to do his best to make sure they stayed together this time.

Tim walked back into the house. Sassy and Thorn followed without a command or call. Tim locked the kitchen door. He turned to retrieve the pad from the table, knowing he needed to make a grocery run. Somehow, not even that motivated him. He needed to think. Doing so out loud hadn't helped. The one other thing that got his scrambled thoughts in one place was his journal.

Tim walked into his den, sat down at his desk, and unlocked the middle drawer. As he slid the drawer open, he glanced out the window. Two cardinals sat side by side on the limb closest to the window. One sang, glancing toward the other as if to entice the other. The second cardinal preened and chirped. Another song sounded, and the two flew off. He and Susan might be like the cardinals. Only if he got his act together and spoke up, things might work out. Taking out the five-hundred-page spiral-bound notebook, he opened to the last page he'd written. The entry was over a month ago. The night that he'd had the hottest dreams and memories sear through him since the park incident almost ten months earlier. As he turned the page back, he re-read his entry.

Susan lay nude on her side. Her hair tucked back behind her ears like she'd worn it in high school and college. She kept looking away from him. Her hands gripped the edge of the pillowcase of the pillow lying above her head. If he inhaled any deeper, her scent would take him on another lap down and across her clitoris with his tongue. She squirmed, thrusting against him until she arched her back, lifting her hips off the bed. One shudder, followed by another, rolled over her as one low moan crescendoed into another, followed by others.

Tim quickly turned the journal to a blank page. He picked up a pen and wrote. Two pages later, he looked up. Forty minutes had passed. His shoulders and neck didn't ache like when he talked with Leslie. Random thoughts and words seemed to roll out of him as he wrote the pages before him. He knew one thing. He needed to talk to Susan soon, maybe before the wedding, instead of waiting until the day of. He closed the journal and placed it back in the drawer

He pushed back from the desk, knowing his next actions could lead to having the woman he loved by his side or lonelier nights wondering if would he get another chance. He picked up the pad from the kitchen table and began moving from cabinet to cabinet, making a list of what he needed to get at the market. Fifteen more minutes passed before he made his way out the door, down the drive, and on his way to the store. Tim hoped Leslie got through the traffic he encountered. Nina wouldn't be happy if Leslie was late. Her parents were sticklers for being on time.

Chapter Seven

"Shit," Leslie cussed, waiting to make the left turn into the housing complex Nina lived in. He had ten minutes to make it to her place. Traffic combined with some city dipshits tinkering with the lights at different intersections across town threw him off schedule more than he liked. Tim's revelation about his feelings for Susan still astonished him. Neither of them had acted like they were more than good friends during high school. College had brought Susan and Tim together occasionally during their visits home.

Leslie eased into the turn, resisting the urge to honk his horn at the SUV in front of him. The kids in the back made faces at him, and he returned a few in kind before making the turn. There could go him and Nina in a few years. They wanted kids. Two of each if possible. Tim had kids and wanted more. Would Susan? That might be a real issue to their getting together. That was up to them. Right now, making Nina's place on time mattered. Her parents compared being late with not being responsible. Thank God Nina dropped that viewpoint a few years back.

Two more turns and Nina's cul-de-sac was next. Her gingerbread-colored bungalow sat halfway down the block. The mauve shutters offset the dark gray front door. Leslie noticed the compact car parked in the driveway as he pulled up. Shit, her parents hadn't listened again. They were supposed to meet at the restaurant. His future father-in-law's stubbornness ranked with a mule sitting on its ass. Nina's mother could rankle curdled milk into crying "stop." Leslie put his car into park, closed all the windows, and combed his hands through his beard and hair. Cascade Bay's mayor couldn't greet his future in-laws looking like he'd driven with all the windows down, letting the wind blow over him as he sped along the highway listening to an all seventies music radio station and singing along loudly off-key. Nina's front door opened as he got out of the car; she stepped out onto the porch waving him to her. Leslie trotted up the driveway, ready to speak when a loud crash and shouting came out the partly open door.

"Clark Carlson, you know perfectly well my mother will be there." Nina's mother's voice reminded Leslie of a blue jay calling out at its highest-pitched warble, ready to dive-bomb anyone or anything.

"Annette, so will my parents. Where do you suggest we put them? Our condo has two bedrooms, remember?" Leslie groaned as Nina stepped off the porch, moving toward him with her hands clenched. Her flushed cheeks told him her parents' argument started way before he got there. Her father's deep drill sergeant voice and tone said he expected to win this without trouble.

Leslie took hold of Nina's arm, pulling her to him. He swept her into his arms, leaned down, and whispered, "What got this started?"

Nina pressed her face tighter to him. He could feel her grin, followed by muffled giggles. A few moments passed before Nina tipped her head back. She blinked, glanced over her shoulder, and spoke. "My grandparents called, stating they weren't going to stay at Mom and Dad's. Then my parents announced they're moving."

"Didn't they move a year ago?" Leslie leaned down and brushed his lips over Nina's.

"Yes. My great uncle left Dad his eighteen-hundred-square-foot home in Vancouver." Nina shook her head. "That's four hundred feet more than their condo."

"What do your grandparents want?" Leslie reached out and tucked a strand of loose hair behind Nina's ear.

"They want to stay in a hotel near the church. Neither of them wants to stay in the sardine can as they call Mom and Dad's condo." Nina stuck out her tongue as more of her parents' argument crashed out of the house into the yard.

"Before this becomes a city-wide issue, let's corral them as best we can and get going." Leslie released Nina and moved toward the house. He glanced behind him to see where Nina was.

Nina hung back, wrapping her arms back around her. "What's wrong?" Leslie asked, retracing his steps until he stood beside her.

"Do we have to go in one car?" Nina glanced at her parents' car.

"Oh no, we don't," Leslie stated. "They go in theirs and we go in mine."

"What started this sardine can obsession of theirs, I don't know. I'm glad we part ways with them after dinner." Nina walked beside him as Leslie started toward the house again.

"Downsizing got it started. May we never get to the point where separate bedrooms is our norm." Leslie stepped up onto the front porch. An eerie silence greeted him. He glanced at Nina. "Too damn quiet."

Nina tittered behind her hand, muffling her laughter. "Well, maybe this will be the capper for the evening, or *we* got body clean up in aisle two, love."

Leslie followed Nina into the house, hoping her parents were in makeup mode or ran out of words to toss at each other. Talking with her about Tim and Susan would have to wait until they were on their way to the restaurant.

Forty minutes later, two cars pulled out of Nina's driveway. Cleanup was minimal. Nina's parents quietly apologized for arguing. With hotel reservations finalized for the grandparents, maybe the evening was looking up. Nina whispered something about an overnight kit in her tote. That meant she planned on hiding out across town at his place. Good, they would have time to talk about Tim and Susan after dinner.

Nina leaned over and kissed Leslie's cheek. "My parents are something else."

Leslie chuckled as he pulled into his driveway. "Now that we know their timeline for moving, you can't blame them for being stressed."

"Yes, and Grandma announcing she's got a new beau..." Nina's voice trailed off as she got out of the car.

"The look on your mother's face when she said that, followed by she wasn't asking permission or their opinion." Leslie entwined his hand with hers.

Nina squeezed Leslie's hand as they walked up the front walk of what would be their home in a matter of weeks. More changes added to the mix now with her parents starting their move shortly after the wedding. By the time, she and Leslie returned from their Hawaiian honeymoon, her parents would be two states away in Canada. That would take some getting used to. Then Grandma and her new fella might keep things lively if they moved into the senior housing complex in Tim's neighborhood. As Leslie unlocked his front door, Nina leaned into him, whispering, "Warm shower, cool sheets, and some hot loving?"

Leslie fumbled with the keys, glancing at her, wide-eyed. Nina burst out laughing. "Leslie Snider, you're blushing! You've never been propositioned before?"

Leslie pushed the front door open. Nina watched him shove his key-filled hand into his suit coat pocket, lean down, and sweep her up in his arms. "Not on my front porch by one of the sexiest women I know. No." Leslie brushed his lips over hers, silencing her comeback. One last thought crossed Nina's mind. Had Tim made good on his apology? Leslie mentioned Tim's text during dinner. Susan probably would call in the morning, needing to talk.

Nina padded back across the bedroom, wondering if Leslie understood her concerns. Tim and Susan's combined past together contained more rocks than smoothness. Tim's reason for choosing Susan made the hair on the back of Nina's neck to stand up every time he repeated his reason. How could he know someone he had barely spoken to in the last seven years or before that? Leslie refused to say more about his discussion with Tim other than repeating what Tim already said. As they talked more, Leslie pointed out that Beth and Dottie's husbands were accompanying them. Logistics put Tim and Susan together regardless of Tim or Susan's decisions. Nina sat down on the bed, sighing as she picked up her cell phone. Susan hadn't responded to any of her texts. No voice mail icon showed or missed call either.

"Stop   worrying,"   Leslie   sleepily   mumbled.   "You're   on   her in-case-of-emergency list."

"I know. This isn't like her." Nina slipped under the covers Leslie held up, spooning to him.

Leslie kissed her shoulder. His warm breath feathered down her neck and across her shoulders. "She's probably asleep. May have muted her phone by accident."

Nina glanced at the clock on the bedside table close to her. 2:30 a.m. In seven hours, Leslie would catch the train to Sacramento for four days of meetings with their state representative for meetings on local and county funds. What a time for the deputy mayor to elope to Vegas with his fiancée! Life went on no matter how absurd or unreasonable things appeared.

"Go to sleep," Leslie muttered, pulling her closer. "You'll get your answers soon enough."

Nina nodded, knowing Leslie was right. She took a deep breath and envisioned her body relaxing from the soles of her feet to the top of her head. REM sleep soon claimed her.

Chapter Eight

Tim glanced at the list in his hand. He turned down the aisle next to the produce section. As he reached for a gallon of milk, he saw her.

Susan stood at the opposite end of the aisle talking with a woman and her toddler. He stopped, letting his eyes drink in the vision in front of him. Her hair was longer. She wore it in a braid. She hadn't done that since he teased her about knowing one way of doing her hair. Her natural color stood out against the peach top she wore. Her pert breasts accented curves without being over the top. The slit in her skirt had him wondering what she wore under it. Skimpy bikini panties like she had in Vegas? He had to get a grip, or he'd be harder than he was two nights ago.

Tim swallowed hard, gripping the milk jug firmly. He placed it in the cart. A bit farther down the aisle, he placed a gallon of orange juice next to the milk. Eggs and cheese came next. The closer he got to the yogurt section the closer Susan got. As she turned, her gaze met his. Moments seemed to pass before...

"Tim, good to see you," Susan said, stopping close to him.

"And you." Tim glanced at her cart. Many of her items matched his. Good, they ate alike. Nice thing to know. Looking up, he caught her grin. "What I'd do?"

"Giving food the once over like you did in high school. You must be hungry." Susan winked.

"Cupboards are kinda bare. Deciding what to add to the steaks I'm getting." Tim placed several cartons of yogurt in the cart. "Any suggestions?"

"Usual baked potatoes? Or if you're okay with trying something different." Susan stopped speaking.

"What you got in mind?" Tim pushed his cart to the opposite side of the aisle. He added salad ingredients to the cart.

"Jeff gave me a recipe for cinnamon-rubbed baked sweet potatoes. I prefer yams." Susan picked up two medium-size yams. "Wash them, pat dry, and rub with brown sugar and cinnamon. Wrap in foil and place in the coals to cook while you grill the steaks."

"Sounds good. What else?" Tim moved his cart closer to Susan. She backed away, looking over the produce and adding items to her cart as she continued talking.

"Of course, salad. There's a dressing that I love to make. Yogurt, a dash of half and half, southwest seasoning, and a quarter cup of milk." Susan started to push her cart away from the produce area.

Tim reached out and touched Susan's arm. Heat leaped off her onto his wrist like sparks jumping from one live wire to another. Letting go wasn't an option. A connection surged, leaving him staring at her eyes and face, wanting to ask her to come home with him. Home and what? A cough and sneeze sounded behind them. Tim glanced down, speaking, "Sorry about that." He let go of Susan's arm. "That sounds good. I've got the grill and the meat. You've got the recipes. Help me shop and come..." He paused, wet his lips and went with the nudge his libido and conscience gave him. "Over for steak and some of those yams and salad?"

He looked away, bracing for her no. Their conversation so far was going okay. Dinner might open the door to talking more. He might get to present his apology in a way that came out as sincere rather than blurted like he'd almost done twice since she first spoke.

"I've got perishables to put away." Susan added bananas and peaches to her cart. "I can help you get some ingredients to make simple side dishes if you tell me what meat you're getting."

Tim exhaled, hoping he didn't sigh aloud. She hadn't said no. Maybe as they discussed recipes and what to buy, he'd come up with another way to get her interest peaked in coming over. "Thanks for the offer. You're on." He listed a few of the meat cuts he had in mind.

"Okay, follow me. I'll guide you through some rice, pasta, and veggie sides you can make. Tossing in leftovers can stretch these, too." Susan started down another aisle. Tim followed, answering her questions as they went. After the fourth aisle, he understood what Jeff said about bachelor cooking. Karlene had used more cookbooks and culinary aids than most of the cooking shows she had watched. From what Susan told him, he could make a gourmet meal with simple ingredients. Was she willing to give hands-on tutorials?

"And that will get you through most of what you've got. Now I've got to finish up my shopping. Been great seeing you." Susan turned, ready to walk away. Away from him without even saying if she'd see him again. Wait, see him again? Lord, his mind was acting like she'd blown him off.

"Susan, I'm serious about the dinner offer." He said it a bit louder than he intended. Glancing around, no one else was in the aisle.

Susan turned back. "You said filet mignon cuts. You need mushrooms for those and a béarnaise sauce."

Tim grinned. "Tonight easy dinner, your yam recipe, tossed salad with your dressing, and my grilling expertise—skirt steaks rubbed with Italian seasoning and sea salt, a dash of cracked pepper, and a touch of Dijon mustard."

"I can smell those steaks cooking already. You learned Jeff's basic rub recipe, didn't you?" Susan licked her lips.

"Yes, out of self-defense. A man has to know how to make a steak tasty." Tim pushed his cart toward the checkout lane. "I can follow you to your place. Wait while you put your stuff away then you follow me to mine. Deal?"

Susan glanced at her watch. She pulled out her cell phone and spoke. "I just moved into my condo. I'm still getting familiar with things. Address, please?"

Tim didn't ask if she meant yes to his dinner offer. He rattled off his address, waiting until she looked up. "How much more do you have to get? I've got to run over to the drugstore after checking out."

"Probably fifteen more minutes. Meet me out front. I'll wait for you if I don't see you." Susan smiled and walked back toward the frozen food section. Tim stuffed one hand into his pants pocket lest he reach up to pinch his cheek and make sure his mouth wasn't hanging open. Susan agreed to have dinner with him. Even come over to his place. He looked one more time in the direction she'd gone. She hadn't turned back or asked what the drugstore run was for. Not that he had scoring on his mind. His teenage ego learned long ago that hasty and fast didn't bring as much pleasure as leisurely lovemaking. Quickies had their place. Not with Susan as far as he was concerned. When and if things went there, it would be by mutual consent and for a period of mutually shared pleasure.

Tim jumped, whispering, "Ouch." His pinch inside his pants pocket brought his thoughts back to the store and checking out. He noted the time on his receipt as he raced toward his car. He might make it back in time if the pharmacist had his prescription ready. Last thing he needed to do was fall asleep over dinner and over-the-counter allergy pills would do that. He hoped his doctor got his prescription called in.

Ten minutes later, Susan pushed her cart out of the market. She glanced to where she parked her car, not far from the entrance. She noticed a red sports car with Tim at the wheel pulling in close to it. How could Tim know her car? She inhaled as her old insecurities whispered up from the depths again. There weren't any other empty parking spaces close to the doors. He couldn't see when she came out if he parked elsewhere.

She rolled her shoulders and focused her mind on more pleasant thoughts, like Tim helping her load her car. Giving him benefit of the doubt made sense. Taking a deep breath, Susan pushed her cart toward her car and Tim. Her answer concerning the evening became clearer the closer to him she got.

Tim stopped a few feet away from her car. She could feel his gaze sweep over her as though he thirstily drank from a fountain. Heat sizzled down her until she thought her ice cream on top of the cart would melt and pool around her feet. She pressed her fingers more firmly against the handle of the cart. Yes, Vegas marked her. God, the man could pleasure a woman. That didn't mean he planned on seducing her. Well she might give in and enjoy the chase…. Lord, where had that come from? Biting the inside of her cheek, she stopped as she reached Tim's side.

"What a coincidence." She began wheeling her cart down the incline into the parking lot. "You parked next to my car."

Tim glanced back the way he came. He turned, pointing to the small light blue SUV parked next to him. "Nice car. Good gas mileage. Hope you got a good deal."

"Thanks. Fits my budget. Good size for the business, too." Susan pushed her cart to the back of her vehicle. She slid her purse down her arm and started fishing inside for her keys. "I appreciate you coming back."

"I said I would." Tim smiled and moved next to the cart. "Mind if I help?"

Tim reached for the bag closest to him. Susan caught her tongue between her teeth. The Tim she knew did what he wanted without asking.

Susan stepped back, nodded, and held out her hand. Between her thumb and forefinger, she held the door remote. She clicked it, unlatching the hatch. "Appreciate the help."

"You're welcome." Tim placed the last of her bags inside. He reached up, started pulling down the hatch. He glanced at her and spoke. "Now as to dinner."

Susan swallowed, blinked, and exhaled. The moment had come. Was she or wasn't she going to... Going to was what kept coming to mind. Certainly, it didn't appear a walk back in time was entirely happening. Neither she nor Tim were the same people they were in Vegas, high school, and seven years ago. There was a saying her grandmamma said about time healing things. Maybe that was what happened. She didn't know.

"Well, since I took your address and cell phone number, you might already know my answer." Susan opened the driver's door.

"I've learned to take nothing for granted. Assuming causes grief." Tim leaned against the back door close to where she stood.

Susan shook her head. "School of hard knocks graduate?"

"Oh, yeah. Big time. Might say I was co-valedictorian a few times over." Tim straightened up and closed the space between her and him. "So steaks and some more of your recipes, please? I need to write them down."

Tim's pouting face reminded her of her three-year-old godson and his four-year-old sister. She leaned over, kissed Tim's cheek, and replied, "Follow me. I'm at the Cascade Bay Condos."

Tim turned to go to his car. He spun back around. "You live ten blocks from me. How long have you..." Tim held up his hands. "Sorry. My mind was elsewhere. I know another way in without taking main roads. All right-hand turns. Game?"

Susan smiled, nodding. "Oh, yes. Right-hand turns save time and yielding on green for the oncoming traffic."

Tim nodded, calling out as he started around her car, "I'll take you in the easiest route from here."

Twenty-five minutes later, Susan pulled into her assigned parking spot in front of her building. As she opened the driver's door, Tim walked up on the walk in front of the SUV. "I shouldn't be long," she called out, shutting her door.

"I'm going to help you with the bags, okay?" Tim stepped onto the asphalt, making his way toward her.

"I can handle this." Susan hitched her purse back up on her shoulder, unlocked the hatch, and reached for several of the bags. Tim leaned in, taking four bags in each hand. "Really," she began, noting the slickness of her palms as Tim brushed against her making his way to the sidewalk. "I can do this."

Tim held up the bags he carried. "I'll get them to your door. Then come back down to wait in my car. It's warm enough if you want to use the hot tub or pool at my place, grab your bathing suit. I've got extra towels."

Susan sighed, knowing he was holding back as best he could. She did have ten more bags to carry to her second-floor condo. With Tim's help, she could have things up there faster. Images of the heart-shaped soaker tub in a certain Vegas hotel swarmed over her before she could take a deep breath. Her perceptions of tubbing carried the context of shared heat and intimacy due to that.

"You okay?" Tim's question cut through her thoughts and hazed vision. He stood close to the building's door, his wrinkled brow and frown evident from this distance.

Susan blinked, swallowed twice, and answered, "Yes, making sure I've got bags the perishables are in." She shifted the bags she held into her other hand, reached up, and closed the hatch. She stumbled, catching herself as she stepped up onto the sidewalk. Knowing Tim intently watched her made her self-conscious. More aware of every move she made. Letting go of the past and how it affected her apparently wasn't over yet. Keeping her cool with all this was going to take conscious effort. Effort to keep her ever hotter libido under scrutiny. Great, what a way to spend the evening. Her hormones sending out subtle—hell, not so subtle—signals and igniting her pheromones to blast invisible rat-a-tats at Tim.

As she put the last of the freezer items away, one thing kept coming to mind—Tim looking fine in his speedo trunks and tank top. Oh, yeah, her desire wasn't cooling down any time soon. She glanced at the counter where her beach tote sat. In the bottom of the tote sat the one item she tucked in, knowing she didn't plan to use the contents. A woman took care of herself regardless. Three foil packets offered extra protection that going without didn't, like in Vegas.

Chapter Nine

Tim pulled into his drive as Susan parked in front of his house. There was something so right about seeing that. Knowing that Susan decided on her own to be here with him mattered. He knew they needed time to talk. Apologizing wasn't going to correct the past. He had to let go of his angst and need for a yes when a no was just as possible.

He rubbed his hands on his pants. He understood why he got nervous from time to time. Unknowns tweaked the J part of his ENTJ personality. Meyers-Briggs had helped him reach an understanding he lacked before he took time to talk with a life coach. What was pinging his unknown meter strongly?

As he exited his car, it hit him. Talk about tripping over his own blind spot, Susan and his years apart. Even the time they spent together in the past had large separation gaps. Their lives took different directions after high school. With college in different cities, they barely saw each other. Class reunions were places to reminisce and maybe renew friendships or acquaintances. Tim turned, facing the end of the drive. He watched Susan walk toward him. Was this the first of many more times to come?

"Hope I didn't get you too confused," Tim offered as Susan reached him.

"GPS helps," Susan responded, adding, "No. I'm familiar with the surrounding area. My godchildren live nearby."

"Glad you followed me okay. GPS and all." Tim chuckled as Susan stuck out her tongue.

"I'd flip you the bird," she said in a lower voice as she leaned closer. "There are two youngsters in the driveway next door staring at us."

Tim glanced toward the two children he spotted playing in the yard as he pulled into the drive. "Oh, that's my neighbor, Mrs. McGee's grandkids. They watch the house like hawks."

"Sounds like my godchildren." Susan turned, smiled at the kids, and waved. She faced Tim again. "Shall we go inside before they see more?"

Tim chortled. "They will. I've got groceries to take in. Two dogs to corral and a couple of cats to feed." He opened the trunk of his car.

"Quite a menagerie. You sure we won't get run over trying to get to the food?" Susan slipped her arm through the double straps of her tote and purse. She reached into the trunk, taking two bags in each hand.

Tim hefted the five-pound bag of dog food onto his shoulder. He shook his keys with his free hand, standing still for a few moments until barks sounded. "Let me go in first. I've got Sassy and Thorn's food. They'll follow me into the kitchen."

"I can follow them so I can put the bags on the counter?" Susan's conspirator wink jabbed Tim right where he sort of expected it—in the chest, close to his heart. Her sense of humor remained intact. He missed their natural pun and innuendo bantering matches.

"You got it. Tabby and Mama Cat will want pets and attention, too."

"I can handle them. If you show me where to put the food, I can put things away while you unload." Susan moved into the garage, following him to the door.

"Thanks. You're on. Once Sassy and Thorn are fed, getting around the kitchen is a lot easier." Tim unlocked the door and opened it slowly. Sassy and Thorn followed him across the kitchen until he sat the food bag down next to the canister holding the dry food.

Susan watched Tim with the animals as she unpacked the bags she sat on the counter. He talked to each dog, patting them and rubbing their head as he filled each bowl. He carried their water bowl to the sink, filling it and still talking to them as they woofed at him with their tails wagging rapidly. Silence followed in between canine munching. Two meows punctuated the next patch of silence. A medium-size calico cat padded across the floor as Tim bent down to pick up another set of dishes on the opposite side of the kitchen. He reached out, petting the cat as he spoke. "Mama Cat is the matron of the house. She came to me from a friend's litter when I got my first place." A larger tiger tabby cat followed the calico. Tim scratched his head before standing up. "Tabby is a roaming Romeo who decided he liked the indoor life a few years back."

Tim sat the bowls on the counter, picking up one of the cans of cat food. He popped the lid, dividing the food between the bowls. More mews followed as he made his way back to the cats' feeding area. He checked their water container and turned. "I'll be right back with the rest of the bags. Put things on the counter for now."

Susan continued placing items on the counter, checking on the animals as she finished emptying the bags. She spied the recycle bag bin hanging on the wall next to the door they entered through. Mama Cat moved to her as she started across the kitchen, mewing and raising her paw. Susan bent down, hand out, staying still as the feline sniffed her. Purrs sounded as Mama rubbed against her hand. A creak sounded. Susan looked up. Tim stood inside the door, his hands and arms full of bags. A smile lit up his face, reaching to his eyes.

"Got Mama's approval I see. The old girl can be standoffish. Looks like you made a friend." Tim placed the bags on the counter, opening the one closest to him. He took out a butcher paper-wrapped package followed by several more. He crossed to the refrigerator, opening the door as he spoke. "If you'll get a couple of glasses, I'll pour us some tea."

Susan complied, wondering why Karlene divorced him. His manners and easygoing persona appeared genuine. Not the fake Karlene fussed about and whined over at the reunions. Susan kept her thoughts to herself as she and Tim put the groceries away with a small amount of direction and banter.

With the rest of the groceries put away, Tim pulled out a chair at the kitchen table and sat down. "Come sit down. I'll start the grill in a moment."

Susan picked up her glass of tea and made her way to the table. Tim watched her with an intent she'd not noticed before. What was going on?

Tim raised his glass as she sat down. He glanced over the rim before taking a swallow. He sat the glass on the table and sprawled in the chair, laying one hand on the table. Susan drank a third of her tea before she set her glass down. She quietly sat, staring at Tim, watching and waiting. Something was up. Part of her subconscious kept nagging her she shouldn't trust him any farther than she could throw him. She laid one hand palm down on the table. Her other lay on her skirt just above her knee. The nails of her index and middle finger traced the hemline of her skirt in short agitated strokes. She counted to five and started again. Fifteen strokes and he sat there as if his mind was elsewhere. Should she say something? Demand an answer? She'd give him one more set of five, and then she'd...

Tim leaned forward, placing both hands on the table. "I was going to wait to say this. My gut and conscience won't let me." He rose and started pacing. He waved his hands as he spoke. "From junior high, high school, and beyond, I've watched you and me. Watched us make errors we could have avoided."

Susan stopped stroking her hem. She leaned back in her chair, keeping her hands on the table. Tim continued pacing and talking. She listened and counted each lap he made. Then he said the one word that caught her attention. "I owe you an apology."

Susan blinked, unsure she heard Tim correctly. "You what?" She picked up her tea glass, ready to gulp, hoping her dry mouth and throat would cooperate with letting her voice her skepticism that she had heard him accurately.

"I apologize." Tim sat down, this time in the chair closer to her. He reached toward her hand next to him. She didn't move. Instead, she let him take her hand between his. Warmth shot off him deep into her palm and sizzled its way toward her wrist. Her nipples were hardening. She bet if she looked down, they'd be peaking like someone iced her. Images of Tim rubbing ice cubes over her clit and breasts swamped her as he squeezed his top hand against hers. Sparks of heat rolled down her shoulders as her memories grew more vivid, remembering his mouth and tongue laving her chilled flesh warm again.

"Come again?" Her cheeks warmed the moment she shut her mouth. Lord, the one phrase both of them used more than either could count their weekend in Vegas.

Tim smiled, patted her hand, and reached out toward her face. "I'd rather eat. My stomach is protesting." Both their stomachs gurgled and grumbled as if in cahoots together.

Tim stood. He leaned down and kissed her cheek before heading toward the back door. He turned, smiling, and asked, "How do you want your steak cooked?"

Susan pushed back from the table, making her way quickly to where Tim stood. "You don't want to know if your apology is accepted?"

"I brought you here to have dinner. Talk about recipes and help me get them written down." Tim cupped her cheek, continuing where he left off. "I planned to apologize in addition to dinner."

"I'm unsure what to say." Susan moved back to the table, sitting down again.

"Understood. How about you think on it while I get the charcoal started?" Tim reached for the doorknob, hesitating. His actions let her know he waited for her answer.

Susan inhaled, drumming her fingers on her leg, contemplating what to say. Telling him no way wasn't exactly fair. He hadn't said, "I got you here on false pretenses." Could she let go of the past's angst, anger, and hurt? She looked down, pressing her lips together. She thought she'd done just that. Left the image of the young, immature male named Timothy who later decided Tim suited him better in the dust of the bygone times of junior high like when he walked up to her at a dance and demanded she dance with him. A click broke the silence engulfing her and her thoughts. She looked up. Tim stood holding the door open as if he kept waiting and hoping.

If she said yes, was she willing to let it all go? Every past indiscretion? Each anger and hurt? Even if some had been worth it? There were parts of her that wanted closure and needed to understand why. One thing neither of them had been good at back then was talking. They said words and mimicked understanding. They hadn't really gotten the full view. They'd come close a few times like today and this evening. Maybe more was in the offing if she said she partially accepted his apology.

Susan stood and walked over to Tim. She laid her hand on his shoulder. He turned his head toward her. She spoke as his gaze met hers. "Partially accepted."

Tim moved his lips, ready to reply. Susan pressed her finger against his lips. She leaned closer, kissed his cheek, and whispered, "Unfinished business. We'll talk after dinner." She turned and walked to the sink where the yams and salad fixings lay. She didn't look up until a soft click of the door sounded. Tim wasn't in sight. He'd gotten her unspoken message. She washed the yams, dried and scored them and rubbed each with brown sugar and a pinch of cinnamon. Her mind raced with how she would start the conversation with Tim. She took the aluminum foil out of the drawer Tim had shown her earlier, and she wrapped the yams. Susan wondered what specifically Tim felt the need to apologize for.

Tim pulled the door shut behind him, standing still until he heard the soft click of the latch. He closed his eyes, slowly inhaling and exhaling like his life coach taught him. Shudders and shivers roared over him. Susan had said she partially accepted his apology? What did that mean? Had he screwed even that up? Her even-keeled tone and pitch reminded him of Karlene... He shuddered again. Susan wasn't Karlene—*nowhere near her*. He took another deep breath and exhaled. He unclenched his hands and focused on the moment at hand.

Throughout his marriage, he prepared for the worst with great vigor. Truth was they probably married too early or had kids sooner than either of them were ready. How did he explain this to Susan? Was it necessary? Maybe not right now. His need to apologize came from wanting another chance. A way to show he'd changed and yet say what he'd felt back from the time they'd gone to their first junior high dance together. Talking was going to take time and effort. Would Susan agree? Yes, maybe things were looking up.

Tim made his way over to the small storage chest close to the grill. He took the bag of charcoal out and spread several in the middle of the grill bottom. He flicked the long-handled lighter, waiting for the flame to take. Patience and knowledge got the charcoal going. Relationships needed the same thing. Patience and knowledge, with these in place, the foundation of a relationship might begin. He had knowledge. Patience—well, that remained to be seen. He started back across the deck, knowing that his patience would need a bit of stretching to get them through dinner preparations. He reached the door, pausing and wondering if asking what he could do to help might start some conversation. It was worth a try. Silence still unnerved him. Karlene's quiet fumes put him on the eggshell walk while he watched and waited. Susan wasn't Karlene. Getting past his past took conscious effort sometimes.

He opened the door and stepped in. Susan came into view as he neared the table. She looked up from the counter where she stood emptying the bag of salad mixings into a large bowl. She smiled at him as he got closer. A glow reached her eyes and lightened up her face. This wasn't his past before him. With some work, patience, knowledge, and discussion, his future was before him, a future that might include Susan.

Chapter Ten

Susan leaned back in her chair. Tim ate with the same gusto she remembered from high school. He dug into the salad once he tasted the dressing, giving her two thumbs up halfway through his first bowl. While they waited for the steaks to cook, Tim brought out their senior yearbook. Talk had centered on who remained in town and what they knew about others from their graduating class.

Susan lifted her wine glass. "To memories, growth, and knowing when to say thank you." She touched her glass to Tim's, sipped, and set the glass back down. Picking up her knife and fork, she lifted her gaze to meet Tim's. As his met hers, she spoke again. "Thank you. Thank you very much."

Tim stared at her. His eyes were wide open. She was sure he wanted to ask why. His flushed neck and cheeks told of his consternation and heat. He cut into his steak and forked a piece into his mouth. As he chewed, Susan cut her steak into several bite-size pieces. She looked up as she speared two pieces. Tim watched her intently. She laid her fork down and asked the question he appeared to want to ask. "Why?"

Tim nodded, sipping some of his wine before he spoke. "Yes, why. Why are you thanking me?"

Susan held up a finger. She ate two bites of her steak, chewing slowly, knowing her response mattered. She weighed her words fully aware of how they could impact the evening and change the mood. She wiped her mouth with her napkin. Laying her hand palm up on the table, she spoke. "Give me your hand."

"Give you my hand?" Tim glanced away from her down to where her hand lay on the table, well away from the items sitting between them.

"Yes, your hand. Place your palm tight against mine. You asked me to trust you earlier when you invited me to dinner. Now I'm asking you to do the same." Susan sipped more of her wine. She watched and waited for Tim's decision. Neither of them could move forward if they couldn't make peace with their pasts and the past they shared from time to time. What the future held probably wouldn't show tonight. Reaching an amicable truce needed both of their buy-ins. They owed that much to Nina and Leslie. Beyond that was up to them alone and no one else. Would Tim help her take the first step toward making the second step together?

Tim's wine glass sat where he'd set it before asking his question. How long did she give him? Did she verbalize the time? Or what she hoped for? The outcome that could happen? Did she know what that could be? She picked up her spoon, scooped the last of her yam out of its skin and into her mouth. Cinnamon followed by a blast of heavy sweetness coated her taste buds as she swallowed. Would Tim taste the same if she kissed him? Touched her lips to his, tracing his mouth with her tongue until he opened allowing her a taste of him. She inhaled sharply as her thoughts grew more vivid. Heat slowly wrapped its tendrils around her wrist, working its way up her arm and...she looked to her left. Tim's hand, palm down, lay flat against hers. His palm lay horizontally across hers, his thumb close to the base of her thumb. He swiped his thumb back and forth over the back of her wrist.

He smiled, nodding as she looked up. "Tell me why, please. We're flesh to flesh. I can feel your pulse every time I brush my thumb across your wrist. You're as warm as I am."

Susan looked up. Her gaze met Tim's. One short staggered breath flowed after another the longer she looked at him. Inhaling, holding her breath, she looked away. She needed to answer him. Speaking the truth, even if it was her view only, made the difference. Her heart and gut would know. Could she trust Tim? She had to trust herself and know that it was okay if errors happened along the way. Mistakes could lead to second chances. It appeared she and Tim were getting one even if it was a minor one. She pressed her lips together at where her thoughts and images went next. That was a memory, right? Not what she wanted here and now, or was it?

She let go of a long exhale, willing her mind to clear the chaotic vision attempting to embrace her. She smiled. Squeezing Tim's hand, she answered him. "Thank you for being you."

Tim opened his mouth to retort, she was sure. Susan shot up her right hand, speaking as she did. "Please hear me out. There's more to this."

Tim nodded, closing his mouth. He squeezed her hand back.

"You gave a damn. You voiced that at times. Crassly sometimes, too. At sixteen and seventeen, we're still learning finesse. I didn't realize you cared."

"Oh yeah, I was a real asshole at times. I'm surprised you or another person didn't slap me from time to time."

Susan tittered. "After Sheena punched you in the arm twice, you changed tactics. By then, you'd already said of some the most cutting things to me."

"That's why I owe you an apology." Tim picked up his wine, drank some, and set the glass down.

"You know part of what you said was the truth. Everyone else was busy being nice. The hard part was hearing it from a guy. Frack, my father never gave me more than a cursory look most days." Susan pulled her hand out from under Tim's. The conversation was going. If things stalled, she'd touch him again.

"What do you mean?" Tim resumed eating, cutting into his steak again with more enthusiasm. Susan noted his energy and interest piqued the more they talked. She hoped things continued along this line.

"After my mother and sister moved away, Dad did what he could. He made sure I had the basics. How to dress a teenage young woman was beyond his comprehension."

"Who helped you then?" Tim continued eating, motioning to her remaining portion. "Go ahead and eat too, please."

"I will in a moment." Susan picked up her fork. "He asked a couple of his women coworkers and an elderly female neighbor down the street."

"Shit, talk about feeling put aside." Tim laid his utensils down, reaching for her hand again.

Susan pulled her hand off the table. "Please don't feel sorry for me. The elderly neighbor helped me remake some of the clothes I found at thrift stores. She had a knack with a sewing machine. The coworkers were the thorns in my arse."

Tim clapped his hand over his mouth. Susan shrugged and continued talking. "Sorry for catching you off guard. They were though. Thought if they mothered me, Dad would show an interest in them. Smothered me was more like it."

"That's even worse. I want to say I'm sorry for that. I couldn't do anything about it. I didn't know."

Susan nodded. "True. Nina hung out with the catty popular girls. She snubbed me until we ended up as college roommates, picked by the university—not us."

"Damn, you had it tough and rough. You came through it."

"Got through it is a better phrase. It took me a long time to come to terms with where I'd been. Nina helped. Quite a few talks and crying sessions undid the dam of held-back emotions."

"Fuck, I added to that dam quite a bit." Tim laid his knife and fork on his plate. He picked up his napkin and wiped his mouth.

"You and others did add some. I chose to cling to the crap that added to the dam rather than valuing me for who I was. Mrs. Watkins, the neighbor, was a retired social worker. She coached me on my visits back to town until she died."

"Mind if I ask another maybe more personal question?" Tim swallowed the last of his wine while waiting for her to answer.

"I reserve the right to not answer. Ask your question." Susan reached for Tim's plate as he asked.

"Why did you cling to my bullshit remarks?"

Susan set the plates on top of each other. She wiped her hands on her napkin, leaned back in her chair, and placed her hands, palms down, on the table. Another moment of truth arrived. Mrs. Watkins had said more than once forgiving someone happened in steps, sometimes in phases. The next step had arrived. Tim deserved to hear this from her. She knew part of being with him at the wedding dealt with this.

"Why I clung to them is..." Susan paused, knowing her next few words could make or break where the discussion headed. She swallowed and finished her thought. "You confirmed things that I heard from others. And I had a crush on you."

"Crush on me? You never said a word." Tim pushed back from the table. "May I ask why?"

"Sure. Low self-confidence. Not knowing how. My self-image lacked strength and a conviction that I deserved a chance. Remember, I learned about men from watching my dad and his lectures on how men were after one thing—sex."

"At sixteen, sex crossed my mind a lot. He wasn't off there." Tim picked up the plates and glasses as he stood. "My mom kept telling me about waiting until I was married."

"Your dad wasn't around much either. He drove truck if I remember right." Susan gathered up the serving dishes and other items remaining on the table.

"Yes, he got home in spurts. He tried to help out with talks and spending time with my brothers and me. He passed before he got to know our little sister much." Tim put the dishes in the sink, turning the water on.

Susan sat the serving dishes on the counter. She touched Tim's shoulder, leaning closer. He turned toward her. Her lips brushed his instead of his cheek. Tim turned more. His wet hand took hold of her arm. He didn't pull back. His lips puckered, forming the kiss she'd pictured as they ate.

Tim didn't know why, nor did it matter. Though part of his psyche said it should. Susan in his arms, her lips and his pressed against each other, and she wasn't pulling away counted. His eyes closed, not knowing if hers were. He fumbled with his free hand for the faucet to turn the water off. Finding it, he pushed the lever down, noting the silence that enveloped them. He turned, feeling Susan rub against him with each move. Her breasts lay against him. Her waist rested below his. If he took a step toward her, her crotch and his would practically touch. Their height difference didn't place them at the level for grinding against each other. Assuming that was on Susan's agenda might get him in deep shit. Better ask than assume. Her hands rested on his waist like she waited for him to say go ahead. Pulling his lips away from hers was harder than he realized. One step back and another created air space between them. Susan's breath warmed his cheeks. He opened his eyes, finding her keenly watching him. He moved back farther, keeping his hands on her arms. He wet his lips with the tip of his tongue and spoke. "Wow?" he whispered.

Susan nodded. "Wow."

"What do we do now?" Tim asked, stepping back farther.

"Wash the dishes? Talk more? Take a swim?" Susan turned the water back on.

"All innocuous. Dishes can go in the dishwasher. Talk is great. Swim may have to wait. My trunks are in the wash. Unless you want to skinny dip." Tim smiled, opening the dishwasher.

"No skinny dipping. I'll rinse. You load." Susan picked up the first plate, passing it under the stream of water, holding it out to Tim.

Tim took hold of the plate, slipping his fingers over hers. Susan winked at Tim as he glanced at her. She looked away, feeling heat rise up her neck, moving toward her cheeks as he leaned close, whispering, "Wanna stay over? Have an adult pajama party?"

Susan shoved another plate at Tim, sputtering to get her response out. "D–do I wanna what?"

"Well, it's ten-thirty. You've had a couple glasses of wine. You want to push driving home?"

"It's only ten blocks," Susan countered.

"And two of Cascade Bay's finest live two streets over. They went on duty at nine. They circle through the neighborhood, checking on their families around now." Tim looked at his watch. "They swing by at different intervals. Your choice."

Susan picked up the bowl still holding salad. "And where do you propose I sleep if I do?"

Tim grinned as he reached into the cabinet closest to him. "With me?"

Susan looked at the bowl, then Tim, and back to the bowl. "You got a yen to wear this?" She smiled her best Cheshire cat one he bet.

"No, I'll save that for another time. Let's get that salad put away." Tim took the bowl from Susan. He emptied the greens into a plastic gallon storage bag. "There's a container in the next cabinet over for the dressing. I like that stuff."

Susan took the container out and poured the remaining dressing into it. Tim watched her for several more moments before taking hold of her wrist. "Thanks for helping out. We can relax and talk more once the dishwasher is going."

He tugged Susan to him. She put up one hand as she came toward him. "Relax maybe. Maybe a chaperone, too."

Tim tossed his head back, laughing. He slid his arm around her, commenting as he did. "We got chaperones, Sassy and Thorn. Mama and Tabby, too. You think they're gonna let me sleep with a strange woman without them? *Ha*! They take their portion out of the middle."

"And where do you think we're gonna sleep then?" Susan laid her head on his shoulder as she snuggled him.

"Why, in my bed. They take their portion out of the middle of the floor leading out to the hall." Tim hugged Susan and let go. Susan slid her arms around his waist.

"I think you made your mind up." Tim laid his hand on Susan's hip.

"Could be. Let's go into the living room. Those chaperones need to understand that a strange woman might be in the house a while longer." Susan took hold of his hand, intertwining her fingers with his.

Tim looked down at their joined hands. Were they moving too fast?

Susan turned to him, cupping his face with her free hand. "You're almost frowning. What's up?"

Tim leaned forward, resting his forehead against Susan's. "Are we moving too fast? Is this where we really want to go right now?"

"Fast is a relative term. We're not done talking. Two adults can spend time together without explaining themselves to anyone." Susan moved closer to him. "Where we end up is our decision, yes?"

Tim swallowed hard. He wanted to sweep her up in his arms and carry her upstairs to his bedroom. Not to ravish her, instead cuddling and snuggling until they decided what came next. Part of him needed to talk about how and why he changed. Did it all have to happen tonight? Christ, it wasn't like they didn't share a past. Enough with trying to rationalize decisions by any other standards other than their own. Where the rest of the evening went was their decision and theirs alone.

"Yes, we decide. Part of my therapy after the divorce was learning to think about others and include them in my decisions." Tim didn't look away. Susan needed to know he'd torn himself apart and re-envisioned himself. Parts of the unsure teen remained. He'd grown into the man standing before her. How much more revelation went on depended on where their conversation went.

Chapter Eleven

Susan followed Tim into the living room. As she gazed around the room, she noted pictures of two teens and Tim at various points throughout the room. The teens must be his daughters, Jennifer and Hailey. Other landscapes and various beach prints adorned the walls. His overstuffed couch reminded her of the comfortable couch she and her cousins curled up on at her grandmother's for late-night conversations and pajama parties that included her grandmother.

Tim stopped close to the windows facing out toward the backyard. His exercise pool and hot tub stayed in sight no matter where she looked as she moved further into the room. He reached for the blind. "If you like, we can sit out on the deck and talk. I'd offer the hot tub. With my trunks in the wash, clothing optional is my hot tub gear." He smiled as he took hold of the pull for the blind. "Then there's my briefs if that is your preference."

Susan shook her head as she answered, "Thanks, but no thanks. I'm not into getting into hot water in the middle of Santa Ana season."

"I get ya on that." Tim began closing the blind.

Susan sat down on the end of the couch opposite where Tim stood. She took off her sandals and curled her legs up close to her. She looked toward Tim, continuing her line of thought. "I'll take a rain check on the pool offer, please. One afternoon soon, we could do a cooking lesson and use the pool."

"Sounds like a winner. You let me know when and I'll coordinate the ingredients." Tim sat down on the other end of the couch. Sassy got up, came over, and sat down next to him, laying her head on his knee. Tim reached out, stroking Sassy as he spoke. "So back to our discussion. We've both been through a lot."

"Yes, we have. You mentioned therapy during dinner. Was your marriage that bad?"

Tim smiled and shrugged. "Bad is a relative definition. It wasn't great by the time we divorced. Karlene and I were dissatisfied with our life together and ourselves. We tried talking it out."

"And?" Susan reached behind her, angling the pillow more as she leaned back against the arm of the couch. "I didn't ask Karlene too many questions when I saw her at a reunion. She snubbed me some."

Tim kicked off his shoes and propped his feet on the coffee table. "Karlene's need to belong overruns her sensibility from time to time. It's what set us on edge a lot."

"Belonging is a human core need. I learned that one the hard way. I think you did, too."

"When I finally looked back, yes, I did. Some of us didn't know that's what we wanted or needed. Karlene sought it no matter who she hung with. Her family was pretty normal compared to yours and mine." Tim angled himself into the couch so he faced her. Susan could tell this was a favorite position as he slumped down into the corner more.

"Question."

"Sure." Tim laid his hands on his legs. He looked straight at her. One thought claimed her attention at this point. They were really talking. Hearing each other and commenting on what they said. A dialogue was happening. Why couldn't they have done this before now? Was this a product of their experiences and work to heal and change?

"Why was it so important that you said what you did to me?" Susan stretched her legs out next to Tim's. They touched without an agenda to it. Their positions said their comfort with each other was growing the more they talked. Was it because they were consciously aware of what they were doing?

"Back in high school?"

"Yes. That's one thing I've wondered about for a while." Susan tugged her skirt down, hoping that she hadn't flashed Tim. Degrees of ease came with trust. How much she would let her guard down depended on Tim's response. She needed to hear the truth. That was part of her foundation builders. She needed to know what Tim said was truthful, even if it hurt. Trust mattered in more ways than she could put into words.

Tim pressed his lips together. She could see he weighed his reply. He earned an extra point for that. Another sign he'd grown. First one was when he asked and waited for her reply; he didn't go ahead assuming what she wanted was what he wanted. Second came now as he didn't blurt out an answer. He thought about what he would say. Clear evidence he'd grown.

"Part of it was I did give a damn as you said earlier. I could see what was going on from the outside. The other times, I wanted to be your white knight. The one you turned to." Tim reached out, laid his hand on her leg, and leaned forward. "Even back then, you got to me like you do now."

His gaze never wavered. He kept looking at her without moving. Susan tried to inhale. Wasn't happening. Tim was attracted to her? And for some time? She drew in what air she could, opened her mouth, and got out the only word she could form. "Whoa!"

"Caught you off guard, too? Believe me; I stumbled when it hit me." Tim sat up, sliding his hand higher on her leg.

Susan looked down to where Tim's hand lay. Close to her knee, not on it, and the question running through her was, why did he wait? Who was in control—her hormones or her conscience? Frack, both of them were pushing her toward the edge of her comfort zone. Taking risks swerved away from her overly cautious side—a side that so far kept her from being hurt. This discussion swung in curves she hadn't anticipated. When had her guard gone all the way down to letting Tim come this close, both physically and with words?

In the kitchen. You kissed him. Did you think he'd do the same thing? That he'd stayed the same? Why couldn't her psyche keep its mouth shut? *'Cuz you know this is what you want and been wanting. Admit it, darlin'. He's the one you've compared all the others to. Mutual desire ain't bad. So why you complainin'?*

"I'm blown away. Wondering why we avoided this discussion before now." Susan leaned forward and laid her hand on Tim's.

"Off-the-wall comment here. Does it really matter?" Tim sat up, causing his hand to ride higher on her leg, up above her knee very close to the hem of her skirt.

Susan licked her lips and took a deep breath, very aware of how much her breasts rose doing this. She didn't exhale right away. She held her breath, running an internal check-in. Each part of her voted yes. Her conscience shot a thumbs-up image to her. Her gut didn't flip-flop. No sweat slicked her palms. As if on cue, her nipples tightened and her clit swelled. Admitting she desired Tim would take them to another level. Acting on it would put them at an additional layer that could distract or enhance what they'd started tonight. In-depth discussions would follow. For tonight, they chose what occurred and how deep things went.

"Not anymore. Before tonight, at some level, it did. Now I know." Susan scooted closer to Tim. He slid his other hand under her leg closest to him as he moved closer to her.

Susan squirmed causing Tim's hand to slip under the elastic band of the leg of her panties. Tim slid the tip of his index and middle finger under the elastic band, caressing her flesh between the top of her thigh and the edge of her pubic hair. He worked his second hand up to the same level as his other. Both hands caressed and rubbed in a tighter, almost synchronized pattern, bringing his touch within a breath of her mons. Tim leaned toward her on his next caress, whispering, "There's a pillow-top king-size mattress upstairs and a lot more room."

Tim slowly extracted himself from between her legs. Every move pulled him away from her, dulling the heat rolling over her. Tim reached over and tugged her skirt down as he swung her feet into his lap. He leaned back toward her, trailing his fingers up her leg close to her skirt hem. He blew her an airborne kiss, bunched part of her skirt in his hand, and waved it up and down. No help at all. Heat swarmed over her in a torrential downpour. What was he trying to do?

Tim let go of her skirt, slid her feet off his lap, and stood. There was no mistaking how he felt. His cock pushed against his pants, tenting his fly area as firmly as she remembered him being in Vegas. Susan looked down, clenching her hands, willing her ingrained past to be at peace with her now. Vegas was another time, another place, and a much younger her at twenty-one. Seven years ago when they met up again, she hadn't understood herself or Tim, much less the male-and-female-psyche dance that demanded trial and error. The punitive stabs to her self-esteem and value were more than she could withstand then. Now, she knew there were no promises beyond sexual pleasure. Could she live with that come morning? Would Tim continue caring? Would...

"Hey," Tim said, his hand cupping her face. "What's wrong?"

"Guilt and memories." Susan wrapped her arms around her.

"Talk to me about them." Tim tilted her head back until her gaze met his. She started to shake her head no. "Please, tell me what's going on. I really want to know."

"Does it matter?" Susan slid her hands down her arms until they cupped her elbows.

"Yes, it does. I'm responsible for part of that guilt and memories." Tim let go of her chin. "I'd like to know what you're thinking."

"Snubbing me when I came over to say hi at Angela's wedding hurt. I heard you tell your date that I was the fat girl who had a crush on you in high school. Now you know."

"I think you can see why I apologized earlier," Tim said scooting to the edge of the couch. "I've got a few things to make up for.

Tim stood, holding out his hand. "It's late. You're welcome to sleep with me. Or use the guest room."

Susan opened her mouth to speak. A huge yawn came out instead. She glanced at her watch. It was close to midnight. The combination of the wine, their conversation, passion, and food fueled the need to sleep stronger than if she'd drank a cup of chamomile tea. Driving even a few blocks as sleepy as she was wouldn't be easy. Tim was right. Staying the night made sense. Where the night went was up to her. She picked up her sandals, holding her hand out to Tim. "My tote and purse are in the kitchen. I wish I'd thought to take my dirty clothes out."

Tim smiled as he took her hand. "Washer and dryer are upstairs. I'll toss your things in with a load of mine. Come morning, I'll dry them as we eat breakfast."

"Okay, but what will I sleep in?" Susan followed Tim to the staircase.

He laughed as he let go of her hand. "My arms if you like. "

Susan yawned again, shaking a finger at Tim. "I mean to wear."

Tim started toward the kitchen. "Go on up. I'll be there shortly. I've got a couple of T-shirts you can choose from."

He paused at the kitchen entry and turned toward her. "Whatever you decide is fine with me."

"I'll get your purse and tote," Tim called out, going into the kitchen.

Susan moved to the stairs. Sassy and Thorn followed her. Both dogs started up the steps. Three steps up, they looked back at her. The dogs accepted her going up? Sassy wagged her tail as she came back down, stopping one step above Susan. Her tail wagged faster as Susan held her hand out to her. Sassy sniffed and nuzzled her hand. She kept nuzzling until she'd worked her muzzle under Susan's hand. She glanced to where Thorn stood on the step watching her and Sassy. He cocked his head from side to side. His nubby tail wagged from time to time. Susan stepped up next to Sassy, petting her again. As she made her way up to where Thorn stood, Tim came out of the kitchen with her tote and purse slung over his shoulder.

"I see you have chaperones. I know how to bribe them." Tim held two dog biscuits in one hand. Sassy and Thorn barked, their tails wagging as Tim started up the stairs.

"Bedroom, now," he called out. The dogs bounded up the stairs. Tim shoved the biscuits in his pants pocket. "They'll be waiting at my bedroom door. Have you decided?"

Susan took a deep breath, turned, and made her way half up the staircase. She turned, exhaled, and answered, "Yes, I decided. I'm gonna live in the moment."

Tim reached her. "Okay. And?"

She placed her hand over his mouth in case he planned on saying more. "I'm here for the night. In your bed. 'Cuz sleeping alone in a strange bed unnerves me."

Tim took her hand, raised it, and brushed his lips over her knuckles. He nibbled his way back across her knuckles before letting go. He offered her his forearm. She laid her hand on his arm and matched his pace up the stairs. She paused on the landing, fighting the urge to turn and look back down the stairs. She couldn't shake the feeling she'd find herself down there staring, mouth hanging open and hands flittering wildly. The old her could stay down there, cold and fading into oblivion, or she could embrace the new, knowing that both made up who she was now.

"I've got two things I need to ask."

Tim turned to her. "Ask away."

"Has Karlene lived here? I don't want to sleep in her bed." Susan started to say more. Her words muffled as Tim pressed his lips against hers.

He drew back and replied, "No, not ever. I built the house after we divorced. I wanted a fresh start. She had a key for a couple of years due to Jennifer and Hailey visiting. I got her key back three years ago."

Chapter Twelve

Susan followed Tim into the master bedroom. Strong male colors greeted her. Medium blues and navies mixed with the muted mauves and golds throughout the rest of the room. Dark teakwood furniture complemented the colors. A large beach setting picture hung above a chest of drawers on the opposite wall. Various knickknacks occupied the top of the dresser. She looked to her right. She noted the open doorway, catching glimpses of the glass-enclosed shower area.

Susan stepped farther into the room. A wall-mounted TV hung over another long bureau. A nightstand sat on each side of the bed. Thick fluffy pillows leaned against the headboard. Definitely a man's room. Well decorated, and hints of feminine touches caught her eye. Who'd helped Tim decorate?

Tim cleared his throat, drawing her out of her musings. He sat her tote and purse on the bureau. "What are you thinking?"

Susan covered her mouth, hoping she muffled her yawn. Taking a deep breath, she counted to five and exhaled. Her mind raced in many directions on how to respond. She opened and closed her hands forcing her thoughts to focus. Two came to mind quickly. As they took shape, she knew this was the way to go

Tim yawned, shaking his head. "Keep that up, and we'll be asleep soon."

Susan smiled, perching on the edge of the bed. "I need a shower."

Tim looked at her quietly for several moments. He cocked his head left and right like he considered her from diverse views. "Let me show you a couple of things before I start the laundry."

He moved across the room into the bathroom. Susan followed him. Her eyes widened as she stepped into the bathroom. Beiges and golds mixed with creams and pale greens across the walls. Thick towels hung from the towel racks close to the shower and soaker tub. Two doors took up one of the walls opposite the shower area. Tim walked over and opened the first one. "Toilet area. Privacy granted with a shut door. Keeps cats and dogs from sitting on your feet or watching you."

Tim opened the storage closet next to the toilet room. "Soap, shampoo, and bathrobe." He reached for the robe hanging on the back of the door. "Hope you don't mind using mine."

Susan licked her lips, shook her head, and held her hand out. Tim handed her the robe. "The water takes a few minutes to heat up." He moved to the bathroom door, taking hold of the doorknob. "You can hand your clothes out to me, okay?"

Susan nodded and moved behind the door. Tim hesitated, starting to move back into the bathroom. She pushed the door toward him. "I'll hand them out shortly." She winced at her tone even as the bathroom door shut. Uncertainty hovered between them. The time for a bit more honesty would come soon. For now, she wanted to wash the day's angst-ridden trepidations away. Sex might not happen tonight. It probably would at some point. When they got there, she wanted it to be a mutual decision.

She tossed Tim's robe on the sink counter. Moving away from the mirror, she let go a soft sigh followed by another. Undressing in Tim's bathroom, knowing he waited on the other side of the door for her clothes bothered her some. Putting on his bathrobe, well, that took intimacy to another level. It was like he touched and covered her nudity, not an article of clothing. She slipped into the robe, keeping her thoughts on gathering her clothes and handing them to Tim. As she loosely tied the belt, Tim knocked on the door. He cracked it open. "You all right?" he asked, not opening the door more.

"Yes," Susan said, opening the door a tad more. She thrust her clothing-filled hand out the door. "Thanks for washing my stuff."

She pulled the door closed, latching it firmly. She clicked the lock, knowing Tim heard the sound. Who she shut out or in didn't matter. Knowing her boundaries were firmly noted sent the ghostly chatter of worries and her past self on their slinking way. She walked to the shower, draping the robe over the towel rack on the towel farthest from her. She put the bathmat down, turned on the water, and padded to the sink. She stood nude in Tim's bathroom, ready to shower in preparation for sleeping with him. Maybe even engage in mutual pleasure. She reached up, undid her braid, and combed her fingers through her hair. Her next actions took on a new meaning. Cleansing her body, she also exorcised her doubts, her fears, and some guarded caution. To embrace the unknowns coming toward her scared her more than a grade B horror flick. Fright led to action. Fright wasn't leading this time. She was, and where she went, she had the strength and confidence to come out the other side intact and stronger for having gone through the experience. Stepping into the shower, Susan glanced at the bathroom door lock before she closed the shower door. Next time, if there was one, that lock wouldn't be doing its job. She was inviting Tim to shower with her.

Tim looked at the clothes in his hand. He held Susan's bra and panties along with her skirt and top. This hadn't happened in Vegas. This was a first. Holding Susan's lingerie changed his perspective again. He'd seen her nude, loved every moment of it, and would again tonight. She'd shown trust when she didn't have to.

He glanced at the bathroom door. Why did Susan feel the need to lock the door? What had he done to scare her? He took a deep breath, turned, and made his way out of the bedroom. He focused on getting the laundry going. Not all the what-ifs he could come up with were going to answer his questions. Only a face-to-face discussion would suffice. He double-checked Susan's clothing labels to ensure he had the right water temperature and cycle. Ten minutes later, he pushed the washer's start button.

He pulled the pocket doors closed, knowing the sound from the washer might rouse Susan. He noted the dogs lay at the foot of the bed. Sassy watched him. Thorn raised his head, wagged his tail, and looked toward the closed bathroom door. Tim swallowed, flexing his hands. Sassy and Thorn seemed to know their pack was expanding. A new member occupied the bathroom.

Images of Susan, nude reclining on a similar bed, rushed over him. Heat deep within his groin exploded in a volcanic blast. Could he get any harder? Anxiety licked at the flames of heat searing him. He reached up, wiping his hand across his shirt. He didn't need to look down to know wet spots appeared. Chills rolled over him as sure as if he stood under one of the central air conditioning ducts. Chills he could ignore. Nervousness came from his past. Experiences with Susan hadn't gone well. Hell, he fucked up a number of times. They were together once more acting upon their attraction. Except this time, lust wasn't driving. Tonight before first light, he planned on making love.

Before another sunset, he hoped his second chance blossomed into a shared romance. One thought exploded the more he hoped. Were they moving too fast? Taking things to a level that would flash burn and die? Fizzle out?

Tim reentered the bedroom, humming a song from their senior prom. The lyrics from "More Than Words" by Extreme spoke to him deep into his heart. He hadn't known then the depth of his caring and a young sweet love for the woman showering. Could she—would she show him the depth of her heart with more than words? Could he demonstrate his without overwhelming either of them and without either of their hearts breaking into pieces?

Tim sat down in the wingback chair close to the bed, staring at the floor. One thought slammed him again. "Too fast?" he whispered. "Is this a repeat of Vegas?"

"What makes you think that?" Susan's voice broke into his musings. Tim looked up. She stood barefoot in the bathroom doorway, his robe tied tightly around her. Her damp hair reached past her shoulders. She tucked part of it behind her ears as she moved forward. She repeated her question the closer she got to him. "What makes you think that?"

Tim laid his hands on his knees. "A repeat of Vegas?"

"Yes," Susan said, sitting on the bed across from him.

"Earlier conversation. Memories. Nagging recriminations."

"Recriminations? Why?" Susan rolled the sleeves of his robe up.

"Vegas set off a lot of stuff—crap in motion. Do you think we're going too fast?"

"Vegas shook us up. It changed us, too." Susan combed her fingers through her hair. "I treasure that time."

"Huh?" Tim sat upright. "I bolted on you."

"No, you didn't." Susan held out her hand. "The front desk called, asking if you were on your way down. They couldn't hold the shuttle if you weren't."

"Shit," Tim cussed. "I didn't say anything." He clasped Susan's hand and squeezed.

"Neither did I," Susan separated her hand from his. "It stung that you left without saying anything."

"I panicked." Tim cupped his hands together.

"We hit and missed so much."

"Yea, we did."

"We're both older and wiser. We know better, I think." Susan leaned back, resting her hands on the bed.

Tim snorted, chuckled, and rose. "So too fast? Just right? Or what?"

"How about as the mood moves us?" Susan grinned, rising.

"There's something to be said for quickies." Tim opened a drawer and pulled out a shirt, handing it to Susan.

"I prefer mutually satisfying. Not into fucking." Susan glanced at him. Her flushed cheeks told him what he said affected her. She remembered the night neither of them slept more than two hours. Two hours in short forty-five-minute naps in between one orgasmic high after another.

"Touché," Tim tossed another shirt on the bed. "I remember you're multiorgasmic."

Susan leaned close, whispering, "I'm here because I want to be. No alcohol talking. I've always been attracted to you."

Tim opened his mouth. His lips moved, but no words came out. His throat had to be dryer than a desert. Nothing came to mind. Even the lingering doubts he had blew away like the Santa Ana winds buffeting the house. Susan wanted to be here. He turned his head and pressed his lips against hers. She didn't pull away. Her tongue met his as their lips parted. The chase began. He retreated. She followed. The taste of her accompanied by the heat rolling off her flowed onto him like rain sloshing down an eave's spout. Thrusts and parlays continued until she retreated, teasing him to come after her. More tastes and soft moans followed. Two soft woofs sounded, rousing them from their desire-laced web. Tim inhaled, blinking, and pulled away. Susan pressed her fingers against her lips, nodding. Tim wondered how quickly he could shower. He needed one if he wasn't going to come the first time she touched him.

"Uh-hmm, I need a shower." Tim reached down, gently pulled the zipper of his pants away from his briefs and aching hard cock. A quick soap down would gain him some control. Control that he knew he needed if he wasn't going to fumble like a virginal teenager.

"Understood. Been a long day." Susan pulled a shirt to her. "Where did you get this?" The front of the shirt showed the old city skyline before Cascade Bay began growing and high rises took up parts of downtown.

"At last year's fall festival. The sponsors gave them to the town council free." Tim reached for the other shirt he tossed on the bed.

"Too scratchy. Got an older one?" She straightened up and scooted closer to him.

Tim held up the next shirt, a soft, well-worn double XL from his first year at college. He tossed it on the bed as he stood up. "How about that one?"

Susan nodded, grinning, fingering the sleeve closest to her. "Yes, this is great."

Tim rounded the bed, taking the other shirt with him. He tossed the first shirt on the bureau. He started pulling his polo shirt off, talking at the same time. "I'm gonna grab my shower now. Give me five minutes." His shirt landed on the bureau next to the other. He walked into the bathroom, latching the door behind him.

Susan fanned herself, sure she flushed from the top of her breasts upward as well down across them. She couldn't hide being turned on if she wanted to. There wasn't a need to any longer. Sounds of water running reached her even with the door closed. Standing, she removed the robe, laid it on the bureau, pulled on the shirt that barely covered her ass. Double XL in its glory days would have been her nightshirt, no qualms no questions asked. Now—well, she probably wouldn't have it on long. She started yawning as she turned back the covers. Maybe she could curl up under the sheet and rest her eyes for a few moments.

Chapter Thirteen

Susan lay on her side, eyes closed. The slow rise and fall of her chest said she slept. Tim smiled and padded across the room, a bath sheet slung loosely around his hips. He looked back as he reached for the overhead light switch. Susan slept on. Good, that gave him a few more moments. He had two items he wanted close by if things proceeded further tonight or in the morning. Condoms offered extra protection. Neither of them needed a surprise nine months hence unlike him and Karlene.

Lube helped ease action if needed. He didn't remember Susan needing such help. Better to be prepared and ready to enhance things than let awkwardness grind things to a possible fast and furious halt.

He quietly re-entered the bathroom. In the toiletries closet, he found what he wanted. He checked the date on the condoms box. Two months left. Good. The box wasn't open. He smirked. So what his luck hadn't panned out until tonight? Some things were worth waiting for, and he was glad he had. On the same shelf, the unopened tube of lubricant lay. As he turned with the items in hand toward the sink counter, memories of one of Karlene's vicious put-downs slammed him. He stopped moving as his reflection in the mirror came into view. He took a deep breath, held it, and laid the condoms and lube on the counter. By fives, he counted, making his way over to the towel rack. He exhaled and hung his bath sheet next to the one Susan had used. He focused on that. The feeling of joy it gave him. He turned, walked back to the counter, and smiled as he picked up the condoms and lube. Karlene found his sexual prowess lacking. Well, toward the end of their marriage, a lot lacked. Desire on either of their parts for many different things including each other dwindled next to nil way before the end. That was then. A very different now awaited him in the other room. And he was embracing it, knowing the future held many unknowns as well as knowns.

Tim flicked off the bathroom light, making his way nude across the dimly lit bedroom. His cock stuck out proudly, displaying his desire and readiness. If Susan roused, she'd see him. She'd know he wanted her. Of course, the items in his hands left no doubts where his thought ran. Rounding the foot of the bed, he observed where Sassy and Thorn were, sacked out on their dog bed curled close to each other. As he reached his side of the bed, he noted the time. 1:00 a.m. The sweet magical hour when lovemaking brought out the satisfying sleep-inducing orgasms. His were going to be inside the woman he loved as they rocked together to a wonderful release.

He drew back the covers and slipped in beside Susan. Susan waving her hand in front of him brought his attention back to the center of the bed.

"Sorry, I fell asleep," she offered, cupping his cheek.

"No problem. I took longer than I thought." Tim moved closer.

"It's okay." Susan smiled, holding out a hand to him. "I got something to tell you."

Tim took Susan's hand. He nodded and advanced, leaving space between them. Susan blew him an airborne kiss.

"I want you. I want to taste you. See if you taste as good as I remember." She scooted nearer to him. Tim didn't think he could get any harder, but he did. Susan's movements dragged the sheet across his aching, sensitive glans. Wetness trailed over his thigh. Pre-cum oozed out, coating him as Susan sat up. She pulled his shirt over her head. He glanced down. Her full, firm breasts came into view. Her deep pink nipples stood out against her pale tan. Their hardness matched his cock. Was she as wet between her legs as his cockhead?

Susan laid Tim's shirt behind her. She knew her decision made sense. Tomorrow, things might change. They'd deal with that then. Tim's statement that their friendship and connection mattered touched her in a way she hadn't expected. Sorting out deeper emotions and thoughts could wait until morning. Tonight was for pleasure and shared desire.

She glanced at Tim. He licked his lips. His gaze was elsewhere other than her face. She smiled, reaching for him when he looked up.

"Lie back. I'm ready for that taste." She laid her hand on his shoulder, prepared to push him down on the bed. She took hold of the sheet covering them, all set to toss it off. Instead, the sheet went taut mid-pull. She glanced up. Tim shook his head.

Susan opened her mouth. Tim quickly let go of the sheet and leaned forward, placing his hand over her mouth.

"Hear me out?" Tim asked, lowering his hand.

"Okay," she agreed, wondering what she'd done wrong this time.

Tim laid his hand on hers as he spoke. "I want you, too. I'm so hard and wet. I might not last for twice."

"Twice?" Susan asked. Flashes of Tim coming twice during their Vegas sessions poured over her. She started nodding as Tim spoke again.

"How about I taste you first? Get us ready for a mutual orgasm. We did those in the past."

Her throat went dry. Twice in Vegas, they'd reached mutual orgasm. The last time the condom broke as Tim pulled out. She'd prayed for weeks that she wasn't pregnant. Fate messed with her for two weeks past her menstrual due date, bringing her woesome worries. Then her period started. After that, she took precautions seriously. Birth control pills and regular gyn checkups topped her self-care list.

"Before either of us tastes..." She made sure her gaze met Tim's. He didn't look away or let go of her hand. "What about STDs?"

"Annual physical three months ago and testing done. No STDs or major illnesses. You?" Tim moved closer, sliding his hand up her arm.

"Six months ago. Gyn exam last month. No STDs or major illness either."

"Good. Where were we?" Tim hugged her to him. Susan leaned into him. Their flesh met. She inhaled, ready to hold her breath, expecting reversion and angst to rear up, ready to bowl her over, taking her back into the dark days of her past. Didn't happen. Comfort and joy flowed. Someone she cared for desired her the same as she did him. Mutual pleasure was ready to happen.

Susan leaned back as far as she could. "I think you mentioned tasting me."

"Oh, I did." Tim tossed the sheet aside as he lowered his arm supporting her. "Lie back and enjoy. Your turn comes when you put this on me." He held up a foil condom pack. Susan groaned. Tim remembered how she enjoyed helping him with that.

Susan lay back. She drew her knees up and let her legs lay open. Tim moved down her side, placing kisses along the way. He nibbled her waist, laving with his tongue over and around her navel. Heat followed by sparks of need bubbled, ready to erupt. Her clit swelled as his hand traced lower along her hip, stroking higher with each caress. He raised his head, blew her a kiss, and rolled between her legs.

Tim looked up, scooting up the bed on his hands and knees toward Susan. He laid down a few inches back from her, puckered, and blew softly.

"Ohh," Susan moaned, squirming.

Tim smiled, reached forward, touching the nether lips of her mons with the pads of his forefinger and thumb. Slowly, he pulled her nethers apart, inhaling, savoring her scent. He glanced up one more time. Susan's eyes were closed. Her hands opened and closed, grasping nothing in them but air. Murmurs and low-volume groans sounded as he blew again. One last inhalation of her spicy fragrance. Yes, time to taste her. Tim wet his lips and pressed his face into the folds of her pubis.

Her clit rose to meet him. His first swipe covered her clit from top to bottom and back. His second and third followed the wet trail he forged. A new taste greeted him on his next swipes.

"Oh yes," Susan sighed, lifting her hips, thrusting toward him.

Tim slipped his hands under Susan's hips on her next lift. Cupping her ass, he licked faster, concentrating his laps on and around her trembling clit. Susan picked up her pacing, thrusting against him. He started another circular lick when she arched, crying out.

"Goodness," she wailed, rocking against him, flooding his mouth with her sweetness. Sweeter than he remembered, with a touch of saltiness and the smooth texture he knew very well. She'd come from deep within her. He traced a finger in the residue leaking out of her and eased it inside her. He rubbed, eliciting more moans and sighs from her. A bit further in, he found what he sought, her swollen G-spot. He eased another finger into her, rubbing in circles, until she began shaking hard, moaning deep in her throat.

"Oh my goodness," Susan cried out, threading her fingers into his hair and grasping his head firmly.

"Easy, sweetheart," he soothed. He slowly removed his fingers, holding still until Susan relaxed her grip on him. She let go as one more shudder washed over her.

Tim pushed up on his elbows and knees, working his way back down the bed. Once he was past Susan's outstretched legs, he rolled on his side. He sat up, licked his fingers, and grinned. Wow, did she taste as delicious as he remembered. Maybe even better. He scooted back on the bed until he could lie near her. "You okay?"

Susan turned her head, licked her lips, and nodded. "I think so."

Tim felt beside him. The foil packet he wanted lay between them. He fingered the packet in to the palm of his hand. He fisted his hand, keeping the condom packet tight within his fist. Rolling on his side, he laid his fisted hand on Susan's stomach. "I don't think I'm gonna last if you taste me too much."

Susan inhaled deeply, trying to sit up. She raised her head and blinked. "I think I'm more done than I anticipated."

Tim chuckled. "Okay. Raincheck on the taste then. I need to slide into your warmth, darling. Help me put this on."

Susan took the condom packet from him. She tore open the foil covering, extracting the condom. She pushed up on her elbows, holding the condom in one hand. "Remember that side position you showed me in Vegas?"

"Oh, yes, I do," Tim offered, taking the condom from Susan. "That is a great way to end the evening, darling."

Tim eased the condom down and over him gingerly. Taking sharp breaths, he covered his glans and worked the condom down to the base of his cock. Rolling on his side more, he lifted one leg. "Come closer to me, sweetness. Let's find that mutual come we both want."

Susan rocked toward Tim as she got on her side. She placed her leg over his, placing her very close to him. Tim reached down, stroked her clit twice, and raised his hand to his lips. "Love the taste and scent of you. Guide me in, please."

Susan gently took hold of Tim's cock, rubbing up and down as he rocked his hips toward hers. On the third rock, two moans sounded. Tim slid into her, filling her beyond their physical intimacy. She swore she heard her psyche sigh and cry out its own relief. Feelings raced over and off her before she could pinpoint what they were. Then there were no other thoughts except Tim stroking her clit as he rocked in and out of her. His lips pressed against hers. His tongue followed, matching the mating dance his lower half performed. More sighs, moans, and pleasured groans followed.

Tim picked up speed, breaking off the kiss. Panting, he mumbled, "Almost there. Y–you?"

"Right with yoouu," Susan crooned. Tim thrust into her and held still. In an almost counter rhythm to her vaginal squeezes and pulses, his cock throbbed deep inside her.

"Ohh, here I c–come," Tim ground out, going rigid against her.

Susan grasped Tim's shoulders, crying out, "Oh goodness!"

Spasms rocked her from deep in her belly down through her womb and into her vagina. Tim groaned with each squeeze she gave until he laid limp and panting beside her. She leaned into him as best she could, kissed him, and whispered, "Wow."

Quiet moments passed before either of them could move. Tim slowly withdrew from her. He rolled away, clasping the top of the condom and sat up. He slowly removed it as he stood. He walked around the bed. He held out his other hand to her. "Let's rinse down before we sleep."

Susan rolled to the side of the bed and sat up. She took his hand. They walked into the bathroom together. Tim tossed the used condom in the trash and turned the shower on.

Susan stepped in, quickly rinsing and washing her face and between her legs. Tim held out her towel, wrapping her in it after she exited the shower. He went next. She did the same for him with his towel. Both towels ended up over the door. "Deal with them in the morning," Tim sleepily mumbled, pulling the covers over him. Susan pulled on the T-shirt again and snuggled down under the covers close to Tim. Soon even breathing sounds indicating sleep filled the room.

Chapter Fourteen

Susan sleepily snuggled deeper into the covers and warmth surrounding her. "Morning," Tim mumbled, snuggling closer. "That feels great."

Her eyes flew open. More warmth enveloped her. Hard, wet, and firm brushed against her the closer Tim curled into her.

"Would I be greedy to want more of last night?" Tim's lips brushed across her exposed shoulders.

Susan swallowed hard and stroked her hand lower, firmly wrapping her fingers around Tim. "No greedier than me," she added, softly squeezing Tim's cock, and letting go.

Turning toward Tim, the T-shirt she wore bunched up, causing it to rise higher than rolling over in her sleep had. Tim came into view, wearing only a sleepy smile. She lifted her leg and moved closer to him.

"Easy," Tim groaned. "I prefer coming inside you. Not all over you."

"Careful there," Susan murmured, sliding an arm around his neck. "We're playing with fire if we get much closer down there."

Tim inhaled sharply the closer Susan got to him. "We can put the fire out again."

He craned his neck to see where the box of condoms sat on the nightstand. He blinked and stared past the box of condoms at the clock. 10:15 a.m. He remembered getting up around four, using the bathroom, putting the clothes in the dryer, and going back to sleep. He snaked one hand out from under the covers, and he held it up as he spoke. "Hate to interrupt things, but what time do you have to be at work?"

Susan started to untwine herself from him. He clamped his leg tighter around her. She yawned, putting another pillow under her head. "Any time I want. I work for myself."

Tim smiled, loosening his grip. "Must be nice. I've got a couple of days off. I could help you..." One familiar trill followed by another, each growing in volume, sounded before Tim could say more. He pulled away from Susan, muttering, "What does Leslie want now?"

Susan rolled to her side of the bed, took off the T-shirt, and padded into the bathroom. Tim picked up his cell phone and lay back, enjoying the view of Susan nude, walking away from him. He liked curves on his women. Hers were in all the right places. Getting reacquainted with those was going to be fun. He glared at the phone on the next ring, touched the answer button, and greeted Leslie. "What do you want now?"

"Oh, the winning lottery numbers and a few extra million to help our budget." Leslie's laughter followed.

"My crystal ball got repossessed last week. You're out of luck there." Tim reached behind him, stuffing a pillow between him and the headboard.

"Dang, I thought accountants had an in on that." Leslie's voice muffled and then cleared again. "I hate to cut your long weekend short."

Tim rolled his eyes and slipped further down in the bed. "I've delayed my vacation twice."

"Sorry, buddy. Dewayne got back from Vegas last night. Your stint as Deputy Mayor ended with his return." A car door slammed in the background. Leslie continued speaking. "I need you and the last two quarters' spreadsheets in Sacramento with me."

Tim shouldered the phone, holding out an arm as Susan got back into bed. "Well, I ain't gonna be there today."

"The finance committee meeting with Senator Reed and Representative Dickerson is this afternoon. You've got two hours to get your stuff together and make the next direct train."

"It's gonna take me more than a couple of hours to get everything together." Tim hugged Susan to him.

"First committee meeting is at four. I snagged Dickerson's time before that." Leslie's exasperated sigh rumbled through the phone. Susan started to pull away, shaking her head.

"Hang on, Leslie." Tim muted the phone, dropping it in his lap. He faced Susan as best he could. He took hold of Susan's hand. "What's wrong?"

Susan leaned back into his embrace, entwining her fingers with his. "Leslie sounds upset."

Tim nodded. "He's in Sacramento for budget meetings. He wants me there."

"You going?"

"Gotta. I've got reports he hasn't seen yet. I'll e-mail him some stuff before I leave."

Susan kissed his cheek. "Can I help you with anything?"

Tim grinned and winked. "Well, there is one thing."

"What?" Susan asked.

Before he could answer, his phone rang. He picked it up. Caller ID showed Leslie calling back. "Oops. Sorry."

"Don't want to know what distracted you. Are you coming?" Leslie's tone indicated he wasn't kidding.

"Yes. I'll e-mail you the spreadsheets and supporting documents we sent Dickerson. I'll text you when I'm on the train." Tim blew a kiss at Susan. She blew him one in return.

"Sorry to do this on short notice," Leslie said.

"It happens. I'll bring the budget reports I'm working on for next year, too."

"Thanks. I appreciate this. See you in a while." Leslie hung up before Tim could respond.

Tim laid his cell back in his lap. "Well, so much for a repeat of last night."

Susan leaned against him, pressed her lips to his, and touched her tongue to his. Moments passed as their kiss deepened, pressing their lingering lust to near explosive results.

Tim pulled back first, inhaling. "I think we best get out of this bed, or I'm gonna be in deep."

Susan clapped her hand over Tim's mouth. "Let's let the puns and innuendos be."

Tim nodded, running his tongue over her fingers.

Susan pulled her hand away. "I need to shower." She flung back the covers and stood.

"Go ahead and shower. I'll check on the dryer." Tim slid to the edge of the bed. "I'll join you in a moment."

"I wondered about the extra showerhead," Susan called out, entering the bathroom.

"I built the house after Karlene and I divorced," Tim replied, heading toward the hallway. "Designed the shower with two using it simultaneously in mind. I got tired of hearing Karlene gripe about waiting to use the bathroom."

Susan leaned out of the bathroom and asked, "Figured you'd head that off ahead of time?"

"For sure," Tim said, giving her a thumbs-up.

Tim paused at the bedroom door. Susan hadn't closed the bathroom door this time. Progress? Maybe. She hadn't vetoed his joining her. More questions formed. Shaking his head, he moved into the hall. One question ignited another like popcorn kernels in a vat of hot oil. Letting them pop made no sense. Worries undermined a lot. He had other things to worry about. Two questions he knew he needed answers to. They would come at breakfast. Checking the clothes took very little time. Setting the dryer to warm them gave them time to shower and dress. Maybe a bit more if he picked up his pace.

Tim heard water running and humming as he started toward the bathroom. Warmth mixed with relief enveloped him the closer he got to the bathroom. One thing replaced any other thoughts as the melody Susan hummed came to him. She mentioned a few times as a teen she hummed or sang during her happier moments. He asked her why she didn't do that more the second time she mentioned it. Her response's gut punch then didn't stand a chance due to the desire and want igniting deep in his heart. Susan was happy. He created that joy and response in her. Something he'd wanted to do for a very long time.

Tim reached into the stream and faced her. "Warm water awaits, sweetie."

Susan smiled, walked up to Tim, swung her arm back, and...a soft swat sound filled the room. Tim jumped and turned. "Not fair," he said.

"Oh, fair enough. Just reminding you of what your touch does to me." Susan sauntered into the walk-in shower, humming again.

She ducked her head under the spray, closing her eyes. The click of the shower door sounded. Sounds of water running at the other end of the shower started. Susan tossed back her head and turned around. Tim's back was to her. She grinned, knowing that if she touched him, a repeat of last night could begin again. Neither of them had the time to linger in the lazy haze of sexual enjoyment and pleasure. Explaining that to Leslie and the committee wouldn't pass muster. "Please hand me the soap?" she asked, holding out her hand.

"Here ya go." Tim handed her the bar and ducked his head under his spray.

They quietly washed in between touching each other from time to time. A few more moments passed until they were toweling off and flicking their towels at each other like a couple of teenagers. Back in the bedroom after hanging their towels to dry on the towel rack, Tim moved toward the bedroom door. "I'll get the clothes out of the dryer. Be back in a moment."

"Thanks," Susan called out as Tim exited the room. She retrieved her tote from on top of the bureau. Locating her brush, she worked her hair free of snarls. She turned as Tim reentered the room carrying a basket full of their laundry. She looked down, inhaling sharply as new emotions flooded her. A feeling of ease, correctness, and yes, right to be here pumped through her. She clenched her hands as Tim turned toward the bed. Why was she feeling this way? Neither of them had talked about where they went from here except her helping him prepare for his trip. She curled her lips into the best smile she could, hoping Tim accepted it as sincere when he turned to face her again.

"Okay, your stuff is on top. I've got to shave." Tim walked away, not looking back.

Susan shook her head. No, she wasn't going to read anything more into that statement than what he said. His thoughts focused elsewhere for now. It didn't mean he cut her off or tossed her aside.

Susan dressed without much thought. She could walk away from this and not let it break her. Couldn't she?

"Hey," Tim called out from the bathroom.

"Yes," she responded.

"Would you mind making breakfast?" Tim leaned out of the bathroom, his face half-covered with shave cream, razor in hand. "Otherwise, it's cold cereal."

"What you got?" Susan asked, pulling on her jeans.

"Eggs or frozen waffles. Also, some pre-cooked sausage patties." Tim hesitated like he waited for her answer.

"Sure. Waffles and sausage?" She sat on the bed, putting on her sandals.

"Sounds good. There's syrup on the middle shelf of the refrigerator door." Tim returned to shaving in the bathroom.

Susan found the waffles, butter, syrup, and sausages. A four-slice toaster sat on the counter close to the stove. She filled the slots, set the toast setting to waffles, and pushed the lever down. In the cabinet closest to the countertop microwave, she found paper plates. She added four sausage patties to one of them and placed them in the microwave.

"Thanks for making breakfast." Tim kissed her cheek as he reached for the empty mug close to her. "You okay?"

"Yeah. Got a text from Mary about a client needing something from an out-of-state vendor. I was calculating time difference and if they had the item or was it a special order." Susan filled their mugs with coffee.

Tim set the half-and-half carton on the table along with a small bowl of sugar cubes. Susan placed silverware, napkins, and plates on the table. Each held two waffles and two sausage patties. Tim put the mugs on the table as Susan retrieved the syrup from the counter.

Tim sat down, spreading his napkin over his lap. He raised his mug and spoke. "Here's to a great day. A superb night and good food."

Susan nodded, unsure how to respond. She raised her mug briefly touched it to Tim's. He sat his mug down and started eating.

Susan picked up her fork, wondering if she dared voice her thoughts. Where they went from here was unknown. He thought last night ranked high. The sex was good. They got along. This morning was going okay so far. "I can take care of the animals while you're gone."

Tim glanced up from his phone. "Thanks. Sitter already taken care of. I got two texts from Leslie as I came downstairs."

"Oh?" She wondered if this was the send-off without saying. "I'll be in touch" and it never happened.

"I've gotta pack and go to the office. I wish we had more time." Tim swallowed a large gulp of coffee. He hastily finished his waffles and sausages. Swallowed more coffee and reached for her hand. "I'll text you when I get to Sacramento and call this evening, okay?"

He rose without waiting for her reply. Susan laid her fork down. Her appetite fled as Tim walked to the sink. Nothing tasted right. Nor felt right either. Talk about a rushed brush-off. She started to rise. He came over, put his hands on her shoulders and spoke. "Finish eating. I'm going to toss some things in my overnight bag and be right back down."

Susan didn't know whether to sit down or flee. She dropped back into the chair and resumed eating. Either one hell of a miscommunication just happened, or Tim didn't realize the double innuendo his words contained. She glanced at her watch as she finished her coffee. Fifteen minutes passed without Tim's return. She placed her dishes in the sink. She patted Sassy and Thorn along with Mama and Tabby, making her way back to the table. She started to reach for her tote and purse.

"Susan," Tim yelled.

"Yes?" she replied, making her way to the stairs. Tim stood at the top of the steps, suitcase in hand.

"Sent e-mails Leslie needs. Admin is printing off the reports I need. Can pick them up on the way to the station." Tim started down the stairs. "Would you mind driving me to the train station?"

"Which station? What time is your train?" Susan nibbled her lip. Depending on which one he chose, the round trip could be two hours. Her calendar was empty. Unpacking more moving boxes awaited her.

"Emeryville or Martinez. Each is about an hour away. I'm ready to go. Two o'clock train is my goal." Tim reached the bottom of the stairs.

"Let's go. It's after twelve already." Susan slid her tote and purse onto her shoulder.

Tim stopped near the door to the garage. "Why don't you come with me?"

"Come with you?" Susan stumbled, trying to stop midstep. Talk about caught off guard.

"Yes, we could stop by your place. You grab some clothes and we go." Tim's grin told her he thought this was a great idea.

Tim sat his suitcase down. He moved toward her, opening his arms. "I'd love to have you with me."

Susan pressed her lips together. Tim wanted her around, with him longer. Her earlier conclusion was wrong. Far off from what he experienced now. "Thanks for the offer. Do you think Leslie is taking Nina?"

Tim shrugged. "Don't know. Kinda doubt it. You know Nina and politics."

Susan chortled. "Oh, yeah. Does her civic duty voting. Discussing politics unless absolutely necessary, no way. And she's marrying the mayor."

"So taking you along isn't going to work." Tim's gaze met hers as she got closer.

Susan patted Tim's cheek. "Sorry, no, it won't. You can call me. Text, too." Susan took her car keys out of her purse. "Let's go. You've got a train to catch."

Chapter Fifteen

Sacramento early evening

"Why do you keep looking at your phone?" Leslie set his menu aside.

Tim looked up. "That bad?" He slid his phone back into his jacket pocket.

"After the fourth time in this afternoon's meeting, yes."

"Sorry," Tim replied. "Karlene's sent texts about Jennifer and Hailey."

"Things all right?" Leslie picked up his wine glass. "Do you need to call her?"

"Probably later. Sometimes verbal is better than text." Tim spread his napkin across his lap.

"Dickerson will be here soon. He's got a late evening committee meeting. He'll fly by and spout off, then run." Leslie sipped the white wine they ordered with their appetizer.

"Good. He went on and on this afternoon." Tim raised his wine glass. "Here's to getting the bond issue on the ballot."

"You bet." Leslie leaned closer. "He called while I waited for you. He's bringing the draft over for our approval."

"He works fast." Tim drank some of his wine.

"I sent him the original proposal several months ago. I didn't think we'd hear back this soon."

"Election year." Tim chuckled. "Also end of fiscal, too."

"Both worked to our advantage." Leslie held up his hand. "Here comes Dickerson."

Tim turned the direction Leslie pointed. Another person accompanied Dickerson. The tall, gray-haired male with him looked familiar. The closer they got, the surer Tim was. He stood as Dickerson and the man reached the table. "Stuart Churchwell. *Long* time no see."

Stuart held out his hand. "Tim, what a surprise. Good to see you."

"Same," Tim replied, shaking Stuart's hand. "What you doing here?"

"Work." Stuart let go of Tim's hand. "Last day, too."

"I'm sorry to lose him," Dickerson spoke up. "I'm in between appointments, gentlemen. Stuart is going to fill you in. Leslie, I e-mailed my copy of the bond proposal to you and Stuart."

"Great. I'll look at it later this evening. Thank you for stopping by." Leslie offered Dickerson his hand.

Dickerson shook hands as he spoke. "My pleasure. Good luck on the bond issue. I'll be in touch."

Dickerson patted Leslie's shoulder, leaned closer, and said something. Tim couldn't make out what he said. Leslie would share later as needed.

"Your appetizer will be right out. Are you ready to order?" The waiter refilled their water glasses.

"Give us a couple more moments." Leslie sat back down. "Stuart, will you join us?"

"Thank you. I will." Stuart pulled out the chair opposite Tim. "I'll have a glass of the house white, please."

The waiter nodded. "Very good, sir. I'll be back with it and the appetizer in a bit."

Stuart leaned forward on his forearms as the waiter walked away. "Let me start the conversation."

Leslie glanced at Tim. Tim shrugged. Seeing Stuart with Dickerson created questions, ones he wanted to discuss with Leslie later.

"Sure, go ahead," Leslie said.

"Dickerson asked me to help out with the bond issue." Stuart paused as the waiter placed a plate of fried wontons in the middle of the table.

"Your wine, sir." The waiter sat the glass next to Stuart. "Your dipping sauces. Red sweet. Yellow hot mustard. Brown soy ginger. Enjoy." The waiter rounded the table placing a plate next to each of them.

Stuart sipped his wine. "My company is closing their branch here. I understand you're looking to expand existing businesses and draw in new ones."

"Yes, we are." Leslie bit into one of the wontons. He chewed and swallowed. "That mustard is hot."

"Good thing we got plenty of water." Tim winked at Leslie, picking up his train of thought. "I see you read the bond proposal. Good."

Stuart wiped his mouth, sipped some wine, and nodded. "Would have out of interest and job requirements. I'm interested in helping you succeed at this."

"What's your take?" Leslie placed two more wontons on his plate. Tim watched him set the mustard sauce away from all of them.

"Small town grows into medium-size one. Land opportunities available. Good schools and location. Prime growth area given location." Stuart wiped his hands on his napkin and finished his wine. "An area I think is worth investing in and a great locale for my company."

Tim laid his napkin on the table. "What does your company do?"

"I'm an actuarial analyst. I measure risk for companies or organizations. Look to see what success or failures they might be facing given the data they provide." Stuart leaned back in his chair.

Leslie picked up his menu. "Eaten here before, Stuart?"

"Yes, I recommend the steaks or seafood. Both are delicious. The chef serves nouveau cuisine that mixes Southwestern spices with Asian ones. A bit of a kick from both." Stuart picked up the menu the waiter left for him.

Tim looked down at the page before him. Reading the list of ingredients reminded him of his and Susan's shopping meet-up. Wonderful food and a fabulous night followed by a delightful morning after. Why hadn't he heard from her? After he talked with Karlene later, he'd call Susan. Maybe this time, their conversation would be more than a few hellos and I'm fine mixed with I can't talk now responses.

The waiter returned on his sweepback past their table. "Ready to order?"

Halfway down the page, Tim found the entrée for him, a seafood and steak combo with two sides. Stuart ordered the same with a mix of seafood. Leslie decided on filet mignon with béarnaise sauce and his usual loaded baked potato.

"Very good. Two steak and seafood combos. One mixed seafood, the other pan-seared fish. Steaks all medium-well done. I'll put this in for you." The waiter nodded and walked away.

Their discussion continued around the bond measure.

"What we want to do is expand business opportunities along the waterfront mixed with residential units. Cay Drive Development has partial funding from the city. With state and county backing, a bond issue lets our town own an interest in the project." Leslie bit into his last wonton.

"I see," Stuart said, helping himself to one of the wontons. "Investing in home turf makes sense. Let's the citizens have a deeper sense of ownership and commitment."

"Exactly," Tim offered. "Folks want and need something they believe in and know. Their money is working for them at home. Not elsewhere."

Stuart nodded. He didn't speak as their waiter, accompanied by two others, came to the table.

"Dinner is served, gentlemen." The waiter placed their orders in front of them. "Is there anything else I can get you?" the waiter asked, sitting the bread basket and condiment tray middle of the table.

Leslie glanced at Stuart and Tim. Both shook their heads. Leslie looked up at the waiter. "Thank you. We're good."

"Very good. Enjoy your meal." The waiter and his assistants walked away.

More discussion followed as they ate. Leslie picked up the pad he had near him. "Stuart, if you open an office in Cascade Bay, how do you plan on billing for your services?"

"Opening the office is a done deal. I signed a lease for office space in the same building as your office." Stuart cut into his steak. "What I'd like to propose is contracting my services out with the city and your bond issuer."

"Sounds feasible. I'll have to run this by city council. You moving to the area?" Leslie forked part of his potato into his mouth.

"Yes, into the Church place on the old side of town. My maternal grandmother's house." Stuart continued eating.

Tim pointed to his fish. "This is awesome. A kick as you bite into it and a tang when you swallow."

Stuart nodded. "I'm going to miss places like this moving south."

"Oh, I think you're going to find Maxon's to your liking. Jeff's cooking ranks with most four- and five-star restaurants." Leslie chewed a piece of his steak. "I bet he could get a few of the recipes from the chef here. They might know each other."

Tim nodded vigorously. "He worked at some high-class European places before coming home."

Stuart smiled. "Good to know. Sounds like I've made a good choice. Thanks for the info."

Thirty more minutes passed as the conversation continued about Stuart's move and when his office would open. As the waiter approached the table, Stuart glanced at his watch. "I've got an early morning telephone conference with two of my new accounts. If you don't mind, I'm going to call it an evening. May I get the tip?"

"Business expense," Leslie said, standing up as Stuart did. "Thanks for a great discussion. I'll be in touch next week to arrange a meeting."

"My pleasure." Stuart shook hands with Leslie and turned to Tim. "Great seeing you again. My regards to Karlene."

"I'll pass them along. Good to see you, too." Tim shook hands and sat down as Stuart made his way toward the entrance.

"He doesn't know you're divorced, does he?" Leslie signed the bill, retrieved his credit card, and tucked the duplicate receipt in his wallet.

"No, we lost contact right before I moved out. Karlene and computers." Tim pulled his phone out. He pressed his lips together, noticing four text messages and two e-mails awaited him.

"I'm glad the judge made her pay for sabotaging your computer." Leslie drank the rest of his water and stood.

"That plus the year's free internet service helped a lot. It all cost her about two thousand dollars to replace." Tim sighed and shook his head. "One expensive lesson." He put his phone back in his pocket. He'd check the messages and e-mail back at the hotel.

He rose, following Leslie out of the restaurant. Getting home tomorrow might be more than sweet if Susan said yes to his question. He hoped she did. Tim looked skyward, his lips moving. His prayer silently rolled forth. Would deity shine on him and answer yes? The e-mails and text messages awaiting him might show what the answer was.

As they reached the rental car, Leslie's cell phone rang. He pulled the phone out of his pocket. Glancing at the caller ID, he spoke. "It's Nina. Give me a moment, okay?"

"Sure," Tim responded, taking his phone out of his pocket. He walked up to the front of the car on the passenger side, illuminated by one of the parking lot lights. He thumbed through his texts. Two were from Susan. The others were from Karlene. One started with Jennifer and Hailey. Karlene's earlier texts mentioned issues with their schools and needing to talk about this. Deciding between Susan and his kids tore at him. His gut flopped each time he reached toward Karlene's text. Susan mattered. So did his kids.

"Damn it," he cussed, looking to where Leslie stood talking animatedly with Nina. This wasn't a quick and easy conversation from the tone and emphasis of Leslie's words. Calling Susan wouldn't be quick either. After two days of sparse speaking, he needed to find out what was going on. Her aloofness on his last chat said something was up. Another day without any messages or e-mails got more insecurities and old issues flaring up than he liked. "Crap, when does it settle down?"

"Possibly never," Leslie offered, coming around the car. "Nina is hot. Christ, what is it with women?"

"You gonna share?" Tim started to push his phone back into his pocket.

"I'm not sure..." Leslie's voice trailed off. He leaned on the car, his phone still in his hand. He glanced over his shoulder and back at Tim.

Tim squinted. The glare from the light made it hard to see Leslie's face crystal clear. Was he scowling or frowning? Either meant shit was percolating. Not in a good way. What or who set Nina off now? "Um, I start asking questions or guessing?"

Leslie stashed his phone in his jacket pocket, pulled out his keys, shaking them. "No. 'Cuz this involves you. Man, does it involve you." He shook his head as he straightened.

"What the hell? I can't be in that much shit. I've been here with you." Tim stepped around Leslie, moving toward the car door.

"Susan isn't saying much. Nina is running down her suspect list and your name came up twice." Leslie bypassed him and kept talking. "You and Susan filled every sentence."

"Shit. Shit. Shit." Tim kicked the tire. He kicked it again, harder. He pulled on the door handle, wanting to get in and keep the conversation rolling. Now getting a hold of Susan started ranking with finding out about Jennifer and Hailey.

"Take a chill out-breath, okay?" Leslie unlocked the doors and got in. Tim got in and fastened his seat belt.

"How am I supposed to chillax on this one? What did Susan say?" Tim inhaled, wishing he knew how to count in other languages to keep his focus on control rather than losing it. He turned in the seat toward Leslie. Leslie's hands clenched the steering wheel like he held on for life. He was fighting with losing his temper, too.

Tim flexed his hands. Angst mixed with anxiety awash in acid slid partway up his throat. The nasty metallic taste in his throat told him the accusation hit him harder than he realized. Twice Nina tried to drill him on his and Susan's past. Now was she pushing Leslie to do the same? Tim looked up and spoke. "Okay. What did Nina say?"

Leslie started the car, glanced at him, and gave him a weak grin. "Susan mentioned seeing you at the market. Nina went into protective mode."

Tim exhaled, sighing deeply. How much did he say? Susan and his night together was their business. They weren't affecting Nina and Leslie's wedding. If things continued along the stressed level they were, it could affect others.

"Protective mode? Why?" Tim watched the city's lights go by as they made their way toward the freeway and their hotel near the train station.

"Hell, if I know. Give me the brief on things." Leslie glanced at him as he slowed for a stoplight.

"Susan and I ran into each other at the market. We talked for a few. She helped me with some recipe suggestions, and we had dinner." Tim looked out the window, hoping that pacified Leslie. Telling more wasn't going to happen.

"Nina grilled me on what I knew. I wanted to hand you the phone. After the fifth it's between you and Susan; she hung up on me." Leslie turned onto the street close to their hotel.

Tim glanced at his watch. 7:30 p.m. Still time to connect with Karlene and get a hold of Susan. The in-depth talk he and Susan needed hadn't happened. Was it going to happen via the phone?

"Sounds like I owe you an apology. You and Nina gonna be all right?" Tim looked toward Leslie, wishing he could see his face clearly.

"Yes, we've had these discussions before. Nina clammed up on me, too. We'll be fine." Leslie parked the car. He faced Tim. Tim swallowed hard. Was Leslie going to question him, too?

"I suppose you want to know." Tim slumped in his seat. How the hell had his life become everyone else's business? Yea, best friends were confidantes and the person that supposedly knew all about you. The back of his neck itched. His stomach flip-flopped twice, and damn his nose started running. Just like he was a kid again feeling cornered and bullied. Fuck, no one did that except his own dumb-ass fears. Didn't getting your shit together get easier as an adult? Apparently not.

Chapter Sixteen

"IT'S NOT MINE TO QUIZ you on. Your story. You tell it or you don't." Leslie shrugged. "I'm here if you wanna talk. At some point, I'll call Nina and sweet-talk her. It's our way."

Tim smirked and nodded. "Each couple works things out their way."

Leslie laid his hand on his arm. "Tim, I'm not making a judgment call. What happens or happened with Susan is between you two. But…" Leslie stopped talking.

Tim turned toward Leslie. "Yeah, I know. If it's eating at me this much, I gotta handle it. And with Susan. That means talking it out."

"Right. Second chances don't always come around again. Making good on this one is important if it were up to me." Leslie shut the car off. "You need to talk?"

"Thanks for the offer. Not right now. You're a couple of rooms away if I do." Tim started to open the car door.

"I'm here for you, bro." Leslie exited the car. "I'll check with you before I turn in."

"I'm glad we're going home tomorrow." Tim followed Leslie inside the hotel and up to their rooms.

They stopped outside Leslie's room. "Home to our ladies. Nice thought to fall asleep, too. Talk to you later."

TIM CONTINUED ON TO his room. If his stomach would stop the incessant wave rolls, his thoughts might cohere. He pulled his phone from his jacket pocket. He placed it on the nightstand. Before he tackled anything else, he needed an antacid. He tossed two of the pills into a glass of water. Picking up the glass, he made his way over to the wingback chair in the corner near the balcony and sliding glass doors. The lights of downtown Sacramento twinkled in the background.

Further off in the distance, he could make out the lights of the houses he'd seen in the daylight. Home took on a different meaning from the moment

Susan stepped into his. There was Jennifer and Hailey, too. The memories with them, time spent together, even the fights added to it. Somehow, he needed to blend this all into one. How was the item that evaded him? Or did it?

An image flashed before him as he retrieved his phone off the nightstand. Yes, one thing at a time. He clicked on his text messages. Sitting down, he read the first one. Karlene sent it four hours ago.

Tim, I need to talk to you soon. School called about Jennifer and Hailey.

Great. His honor roll college-prep daughters were up to something. Last year, they'd been on probation in the form of after-school work helping the janitor repaint part of the locker room. Using indelible markers to write slogans on the walls wasn't such a smart idea. That one he even applauded. They'd struck up friendships with some kids bused in from other schools at the start of the school year. A few gang turf fights broke out. Jennifer decided she liked one of the boys and wanted to go steady. Hailey had kept her head about her until the boy's cousin started attending school there, too. Karlene handled the situation with him from afar. He hated being a hands-off father. Still, going down to San Diego every time stuff happened, he couldn't do. Talking to Hailey and Jennifer worked to a point. They needed hands-on parents.

He scrolled to Karlene's second message.

Second call from the school. Please call me as soon as you get this.

Tim glanced at his watch. 8:15 PM. There was no way he could judge how long the call with Karlene would take. Did he text Susan, saying he'd call after he talked with Karlene? Or call her and say he'd call back? He glanced down, noting the next message was also from Karlene. He opened it, bracing for a few cuss words about why he hadn't called.

Talked to Nina. Know you're in Sacramento. Call when you get in. Urgent!

Urgent decided his next move. His kids needed him whether they liked it or not. Calling Karlene took precedence. He'd explain to Susan when they talked. Maybe tomorrow when he got home, they could get together. Time to let go of the past might be behind them after their last talk. He'd apologized like his conscience poked him to do. Their chemistry and attraction remained strong. Could they move into the present and work on increasing the success of their second chance? His answer was yes. What would Susan's response be?

"Hello." Karlene sounded winded. Tim held the phone away from his ear, checking the volume.

"Sorry, it took a while to call." Tim slumped into the chair, toeing off his shoes. Comfort mattered as there was no telling how long the conversation might take.

"It's all right. After I found out you're in Sacramento, it made sense why you hadn't called or texted." Karlene sounded clearer, less muffled as she finished speaking.

"What's going on with Jennifer and Hailey?" Tim asked, knowing keeping the discussion focused might help move it along.

Karlene's snort came through loud and clear. "Give me a moment. I'm in the car after dropping Mom off at her place."

"How's she doing?" Tim ran into his ex-mother-in-law from time to time. She graciously spoke to him with all the politeness of a dragoness waiting to flambé her next victim.

"Not handling Uncle Henry's death well. Something about her own mortality and a few other mutters." Karlene's voice took on a distant sound again.

"You got me on speaker?"

"Yes. Bluetooth died on me. Got to obey the law about using handheld items while driving." Karlene's laugh brushed against his ear. He'd caught her in a decent mood.

"The two calls from the school. What's with that?" Tim propped his feet up on the bed.

"*Gangbangers.* More busing and now the school is talking about busing students from North Park across town. Less *desirable* schools, too." Karlene's tone had taken on a harsh edge.

"Doesn't sound good." Tim lowered his feet and scooted forward to the edge of the chair. He glanced at the desk. A pen and pad lay on top. He rose, walked to the desk, taking the desk chair with him. He sat down and picked up the pen. Depending on Karlene's response, he probably needed notes.

"It's not. Jennifer's GPA slipped two points. Hailey failed math and science. Both are facing academic discipline if their grades slip more. Then there's the group they hang with."

Tim rolled his eyes. He rubbed the area between his eyes along his forehead with his index finger and the middle finger of his left hand. Taking one then another deep breath followed by deep exhales, he waited to voice his reaction.

Jennifer and Hailey were at fault. Not Karlene. Damn it, the girls were old enough to know about consequences.

"Crap! Jennifer knows her grades need to stay up. She still wants to go to med school, right?"

"That's Hailey. Jennifer is saying all she needs is high school."

"Fuck!" Tim gripped the pen harder. He'd lost touch with his daughters because he let them decide when they called and what they discussed. Maybe a trip to San Diego wasn't such a bad idea.

"Take it easy. Jennifer changed her mind right before school started and the Diaz boy started hanging around." Karlene's exasperated sigh came through loud and clear. The edgy pitch and strength of it told him more than if they were face-to-face.

"And Hailey?" Tim scribbled down a few choice comments about his fifteen-year-old's attraction to bad boys, especially gang members.

"When Roman started hanging out with Diaz—let's just say trouble follows in packs."

"Double shit!" Tim rose, began pacing, and muttering.

"Take a breath!" Karlene shouted.

"Sorry," Tim apologized.

"They're going to make mistakes. Some we have to let them do. Remember what we were like at their ages."

"Oh man, don't remind me." Tim rolled his eyes as he dropped onto the bed. "So we're gonna let them fuck up? Then what?"

He swore he heard Karlene's teeth-gritting even though she was far away from the speaker.

"Counting to a hundred will take too long. So I'm gonna say, no, we don't let them fuck up. Make some mistakes, yes. Major foul-ups...not if we can help it." Karlene's tone conveyed her frustration as loudly as his cussing and pacing did.

"Okay, I get it." Tim combed his hands through his hair. "God, I feel like a piss-poor father."

Karlene's laugh didn't help. "Before you blow a gasket, I messed up, too. Fouled up royally at times."

"We both did." Tim cradled the phone to his ear. "We did the best we could given our circumstances. We've got to unite from now on."

"Yes, we do. Hear me out, okay?" He'd never heard Karlene use a timid tone before. What was with her?

"All right. I'm listening." Tim got up off the bed and made his way back to the chair in the corner. Lord, his sweet tooth kicked into high gear when he and Karlene went at it. Must be all the energy they exerted with their intense discussions. Tim clapped his hand over his mouth lest Karlene think he was laughing at her and her idea. What a time for his absurd sense of humor and lack of decent sleep to join forces.

"Uncle Henry left me the house. I'm debating on moving back to Cascade Bay. The girls aren't going to be happy about it. I need you in San Diego with me since we've got joint custody. It's going to take both of us to sign them out of school." Karlene's voice trailed off.

Tim kept quiet. Words started piecing together. Karlene up close and personal again. Jennifer and Hailey sullen and pissed at both of them. Sometimes you did what you needed to and worked through the impacts afterward. "Sounds like I'm making a trip to San Diego. I need a day to get things set up. Leslie will approve the time off. How long do you think this will take?"

"Not sure. Maybe three to four days. I've got a neighbor looking after Jennifer and Hailey. I asked her to get them ready to come up here. They're balking at it." Karlene's connection started to break up. "My battery's running out. Forgot my charger. Call me tomorrow when you get back. Thanks."

Tim opened his mouth to confirm. Crackling static followed by a hollow pop sounded and then his phone beeped, indicating the call ended. Taking a deep breath, he texted Leslie to see if he was available to talk. He replied yes. After a few more messages, Tim walked into the bathroom. His mirrored reflection made him snicker and snort. His hair stood up in places all over his head. He squinted as the overhead lights got brighter. He looked like he needed three days of sleep thanks to the dark circles under his eyes. The antihistamines he brought with him barely relieved his allergies. Now another trip and between Karlene, two sullen pissed teenagers—Lord help him if their periods happened—and San Diego's weather. Frack, he'd need a week to recover. He still needed to call Susan. He splashed water on his face, combed his hands through his hair as best he could and placed allergy eye drops in his eyes. Maybe he could convince Leslie to give him another week off. For now, he needed to bring Leslie up to date and see about possibly calling Susan.

He walked out of the bathroom glanced around the room patting his pockets. He noted the room key lying next to his phone on the bed. He started toward them. The room door rattled as a hard knock sounded. Tim peered out the peephole. Leslie stood outside, his fist raised ready to knock again.

"Hang on," Tim called out, unlocking the door. He opened the door, hoping he wasn't grimacing. He started to grin. Leslie knew him well enough to know he'd faked it. Looking less than pleased would have to do. Best he could muster given his conversation with Karlene.

"Sounded like you could use a drink," Leslie said, holding up two beer bottles as he entered.

Tim licked his lips. Sweat ran down the neck of the bottles, pooling around Leslie's fingers and over them onto the rest of the bottle. The lettering not covered by Leslie's hands indicated he'd chosen dark beer. Tim looked up, nodded, and replied, "You got the good stuff. No root beers this time."

"Dude, you used Karlene's name twice in your texts. That told me you weren't dealing with great news." Leslie sat the beers down on the bureau. "Get a couple of glasses. I've got snacks coming up."

"You think this is going to take long?" Tim stepped into the bathroom, picked up two plastic cups, and followed Leslie back across the room.

Leslie took one of the cups. He filled it and sat down in the desk chair. "No. Beer on an empty stomach goes straight to your head."

"True. I need to keep focused. What snacks did you get?" Tim dropped into the corner chair.

"Chips, cheese and crackers, and cookies." Leslie raised his glass. "Here's to getting Karlene talked out."

Tim set his glass on the table next to him. "That's a high-end job if you think that will happen tonight."

"Not plausible. Nina called back, mentioned she and Susan ran into Karlene at the new coffee and pastry shop on Third Street." Leslie drank part of his beer.

"Dare I ask what happened?" Tim saluted Leslie with his cup and drank.

Another knock sounded. Leslie rose. "That's the snacks. Hang on a moment."

Tim swallowed a large gulp of beer. Great, Karlene running into Susan. How much did this figure into Susan's aloofness? It was like he was involved with both of them. One he was for sure and wanted more. The other, his ex, well she could get on with the parts of her life that didn't involve Hailey and Jennifer.

Chapter Seventeen

Leslie set the tray on the desk.

"Looks good." Tim rose and helped himself to the snacks, filling one of the small paper plates on the tray. "Good beer needs great snacks. Good choices."

"Thanks. So what's going on with Karlene?" Leslie bit into a chip.

"Problems with the girls. She's pulling them out of the school they're in. I've got to be there, too, since we've got joint custody." Tim drank more of his beer.

"Okay. What Nina said makes sense."

Tim could feel his heart pound a bit more and his hand gripped his cup tighter. Not more shit stirred up. Karlene could be a terror when her tunnel vision kicked in. "Yours to tell?"

"For sure since it involves what we're talking about. Karlene walked right up to the table, gave Susan the once over, turned to Nina, and asked if she knew where you were." Leslie set his plate down.

"How would Nina know?" Tim stuffed half a cracker and cheese in his mouth and chewed. He didn't want to start cussing again. A full mouth would keep him from badmouthing anyone.

"Receptionist told Karlene we—you and me—were out of town. She thought Nina and I would be in contact."

Tim downed more of his beer, wiped his mouth, and spoke. "How bad did Karlene go off on Susan?"

"Nothing verbal. Just stared at her and glared from time to time when Nina didn't answer fast enough for her." Leslie shook his head. "So give me the quick and easy on what you need to talk about."

"Karlene, my daughters, and Susan." Tim walked over to the desk and refilled his plate. "I've gotta go to San Diego. Hailey and Jennifer are hanging out with gangbangers and not seeing the shit for the façade in front of them."

"Got ya. Karlene won't take no for an answer?" Leslie handed Tim a cookie.

"Ain't that. Joint custody requires both of us to withdraw them. The kicker is Karlene mentioned something about moving back." Tim poured the last of his beer into his cup.

"Oh man, that is gonna be a huge maelstrom." Leslie bit into his cookie.

"Sullen teens, cantankerous ex, and a possible second chance with Susan." Tim tossed the empty bottle into the wastebasket near him. "How much more can I pile on this rocky shifting sand tower?"

Leslie chuckled. Tim scowled. Leslie held up his hand. "Easy, bro. I'm not laughing at you. It's ironic you of all folks have this going down."

Tim shot Leslie a weak grin. "Yes, who'd think I'd have this ruckus to deal with. So can I have another week off?"

Leslie snorted, swiftly held a napkin up to his mouth, and quickly shook his head.

"Come on, Leslie. I've—" Tim couldn't finish speaking because Leslie cut him off.

"You caught me with a mouthful. A week off isn't a problem. How soon?"

"Right away. Karlene's made up her mind she's pulling Jennifer and Hailey out of school. Sooner this is done, the faster I'm back." Tim took the last bite of his cookie as he stared at Leslie.

Several silent moments passed while Leslie consumed his cheese and crackers, washed down with swigs of beer. He looked down. Tim moved to the edge of the chair. What happened to accomplishing things easily? The urge to cuss and pace tingled his feet. Patience was a virtue he didn't have much of now.

"Stop looking like you want to throttle me." Leslie downed the last of his beer.

"Well, what do you expect? I need an answer. You know how Karlene is." Tim stuffed two chips in his mouth.

"I do. You're letting her drive right now. Do you have a plan?" Leslie tossed his cup and empty bottle in the trash.

Tim wiped his sweaty palms down his pants and leaned forward, lacing his fingers together. "Not really."

"Wouldn't one blow off the angst? Empower you instead of Karlene or even Jennifer and Hailey?" Leslie leaned back in the desk chair.

"Damn, man, how could you see that and I couldn't?" Tim tossed his napkin and paper plate in the trash.

"I'm not in the middle. Nina even said she told Karlene she wasn't your keeper. So want to strategize?" Leslie turned toward the desk.

Tim sat down on the side of the bed close to the desk. "For sure. You write, please?"

Leslie laughed again. "Don't dictate too fast."

"Got ya. I need to pace to think right now." Tim stood and started moving up and down the space between the bed and bureau to the edge of the bathroom door and back.

Tim shot off ideas. Leslie wrote without replying. Ten minutes later, Leslie tapped the pad. "I think you got a good plan worked out. First, you get a hold of Susan."

"Yes. Important item. Second, I book a plane ticket from San Francisco to San Diego. Karlene will want to travel together. I can't handle that much togetherness with her."

Leslie chortled. "Understood! She is a powder keg at times."

"She's mellowed some. With the girls, she is a first-rate mother hen. Given what's going on, I don't blame her." Tim sat down on the side of the bed again.

"Want me to drive you to San Francisco?" Leslie put the pen and pad on the desk.

"Maybe. I hope to get Susan to take me. I'd like a couple of days with her before I leave." Tim held up his crossed fingers. "There's a lot of what-ifs riding on that."

"For sure." Leslie stood, stretched, and moved closer to Tim. "I'm off to bed. Tomorrow we'll take care of the plane tickets and your hotel reservations."

Tim slid his arm across Leslie's shoulders, hugging Leslie to him. "Thanks for listening. The beer and snacks, too. I'm mellowing out."

"No problem. We're besties, and that's what we do for each other." Leslie stepped away. "Sleep well. Train leaves at eleven. Meet me downstairs around nine for breakfast."

"You bet. I'm going to call Susan and turn in." Tim followed Leslie to the door.

Leslie turned to him again. "Good night. Remember, empower you, not Karlene."

Tim nodded, opening the door. "Sometimes easier said than done. Main point is keeping my cool."

"Yes, she can be hardheaded. Glad she's not my ex." Leslie smiled and walked out the door.

Tim shut the door, locking it and clicking off most of the lights in the room as he made his way back to the bed. The nightstand clock showed 9:45 p.m.

He might be able to reach Susan. He could finish packing in the morning. He tossed his clothes on the chair, pulled back the blanket and sheet, and lay nude on the bed. Picking up his cell phone, he scrolled to Susan's text. Her answers were short without much content. To be expected, texts didn't allow for much. Next, he checked her e-mails. They contained brief responses to his questions and some insight to her activities with clients and settling into her condo. The lines of communication remained open. Shallow as their chatter was, he knew reading more into the texts or e-mails made no sense. Why was he reluctant to call and ask her to meet him at the train, spend the day and night with him? Even go to San Francisco with him? Why not San Diego? Part of it could be his conversation with Karlene and Susan asking about his divorce. Susan and Karlene's encounter ranked high on the list, too.

Checking the time, Tim dialed Susan's number. He needed to face whatever anxiety and fear his mind pulled out to toss at him. Experience said one thing, moving forward another. This wasn't time to get caught up in recriminations. Talking was critical. One ring, two rings, and a sleepy voice answered.

"Hello," Susan murmured.

"Hi sweetie," Tim shifted against his pillows, breathing easier. She'd answered.

"Hi yourself," Susan replied, yawning. "Sorry. Busy day. How's the meetings going?"

"Good. Got what we came for accomplished." Tim gripped his phone harder. Was their conversation going to be nonchalant or focused? "I got a question for you."

"Okay." Susan's tone warmed. Good.

"I get back tomorrow. Pick me up at the train station?" Tim held the phone snugger to his ear. His grip on the phone tightened.

"What about Leslie?" Susan's voice perked up.

"Nina is picking him up. I want to spend time with you. I miss you." Tim sat up, wondering if this might be the time to discuss Karlene.

"Thanks. I've missed you, too." Susan's yawn reminded him of their coziness, cuddled up together in bed.

Tim flipped the sheet over him, covering his hardening cock. Telephone sex wasn't an option, or was it? He slumped lower in the bed, settling back against his pillows. "Your text and e-mails said you were hopping from one client meeting to another."

"Yes!" Susan exclaimed. "Jeff landed catering contracts for the wine festivals in Napa and Sonoma."

"Nice going for him!" Tim replied. "That alone will help business. Congrats!"

"Thanks. Mary had another wedding book with her, so I took over her other meetings. Rushing around is tiring." Susan yawned again.

"Sweetie, are you in bed?" Tim asked, shouldering his phone to his ear.

"Not yet. Fell asleep on the couch watching the news."

"So can you pick me up tomorrow? I'd love to see you." Tim crossed his fingers, rolled his eyes heavenward, and silently mouthed, *please*.

"Train arrives when?"

"Around one."

"Let me check my schedule. Hang on." Susan's voice faded. Tim heard beeps and bits of noise that sounded like the TV playing in the background. "Okay." Her voice came back louder than before. "I'm free the rest of the day so that works."

"Great. I appreciate you doing this." Tim yawned, ready to say more when his phone beeped. He pulled the phone away from his ear. Glancing down, he grimaced. The low battery indicator flashed across his screen. He held the phone to his ear, ready to say something when Susan spoke.

"You're welcome. I need to go to the bathroom. I'll see you tomorrow. Bye." Susan's voice trailed off like she waited for a reply.

Tim opened his mouth to respond when a shrill beep sounded. Shit, a dead battery. No chance to respond or call back until his phone charged. That would take three to four hours, in the middle of the night. Any more discussion would have to wait until they were face-to-face tomorrow.

Chapter Eighteen

Susan glanced at her watch. 11:45 a.m. The trip to Emeryville took forty minutes with no traffic. Friday at lunchtime meant traffic and people heading out of town for the weekend. With no other word from Tim, not even a text, she had only the train schedule to go by. The 1:30 p.m. train was the closest to the time he said. Arriving close to that meant leaving now. Picking her tote and purse up off her desk, she glanced at the wipe board spreadsheet she and Mary laid out that morning. A week and a day until Nina and Leslie's wedding. Where had the time gone? Between new clients, the time with Tim, and unpacking her new place, days flew by. Now slipping into a slower pace felt weird, like she missed something or someone. As she walked out of her office, she waved to Mary, who sat at the front while their receptionist took lunch.

"I'm off to Emeryville," Susan stated, stopping close to the front door.

"Good luck with traffic. Last report said the inland freeway lanes were open. Hope Tim's train is on time." Mary cupped her chin with her hands as she leaned forward.

Susan sighed. "I do, too."

"Something wrong?" Mary asked, sitting up.

"Yea and nay. We've been so busy. At times, I didn't miss him. Others I did." Susan turned back to the door.

"The connection isn't firm yet," Mary stated.

Susan blinked, looked down, and turned around. "What?"

"Yours and Tim's connection. Sure, you know each other, but the tenuousness of it leaves doubts and gaps." Mary saluted her with her glass of orange juice.

"It's that obvious?" Susan forced her next words back down her throat. Mary couldn't have stated the obvious more succinctly. Why deny what she saw? "To me...yes. To someone who doesn't know all of it, no. Confusion comes through for them. They don't see past their own fence." Mary set her glass down.

"Maybe mine blinded me. So much isn't said. The past might be where we've tried too hard." Susan palmed her keys against her hip, not wanting to wipe them down her pant leg. Nerves belonged inside, not out where all could see them.

Mary stood, moving from behind the reception desk as she spoke. "The past can't change. You and Jeff showed me that. It's part of who we are today. We're stronger. Know ourselves better."

"Christ, you have a way of saying what I can't find the words for. Damn, are you reading my mind again?" Susan met Mary halfway across the lobby.

Mary held her arms out. Susan stepped into her embrace. Mary hugged her tightly and moved back. "No mind-reading that isn't my own. Maybe we both need to hear these words. Maybe these men are in our lives because second chances are worth going for."

Susan knuckled a tear away from her nose. She nodded. "Time to let go of the past and the fear that holds us there, sister?"

"Not marinate in it any longer for sure. Our past lessons taught us many things. I'm battling with are we able to grow and see the new path." Mary pointed toward the door. "Go. You've got a good man waiting. Hear Tim out and speak your truth. Listen to your heart."

Susan blinked, wanting to hug Mary again. Nina might have offered similar words of encouragement if she wasn't so close to what was going on. Sometimes the person outside the circle could see more than the participants did. "Thanks. I'll do my best."

Mary pointed at the door again, waving with her other hand. "Get going. Jeff put a sandwich in your car when he left a bit ago. There's a soda next to it. Alexa left the CD for you. Something about love songs and singing out loud with the windows down."

Susan burst out laughing. "She found her mother's eighties love songs CD. I told her I used to drive to school with the windows down singing to those."

Mary chuckled. "Then go serenade the wind and the highway. Enjoy yourself."

Susan waved and trotted out the door. Newness might be scary. The past clouded the mind based on experience. Had she lived and learned to only repeat the same mistake again? Or was it different this time? Shaking her head, she opened her car door.

Inside on the seat, wrapped in blue-and-gold paper with Maxon's logo, lay her sandwich. Jeff's handwriting stood out on the label. He fixed one of her fave sandwiches for her, grilled black forest ham with pepper jack cheese on black rye with aioli garlic mayo. The bottle lying next to it glistened as the sun hit it. Jeff's home-brewed birch beer. Lord, the man hit her sweet spot. She moved the items to the passenger seat as she got in. She spotted Alexa's CD and the note attached to it lying on the seat. Susan laughed harder as she read the note.

Turn the volume up, Mom says, and belt out the hits like no one can hear you. Me, I say sing on key and remember to keep your eyes on traffic.

One last look at her watch said time waited for no one. Tim offered her a second chance that she wished for in the past. Dreamt of in recent years. Now had the opportunity to snag it. Was she going to let this one pass? No, she wasn't.

In-city traffic and a stop for gas delayed her longer than she liked. Tim would have to wait if the train got in early. Susan popped the CD in, opened the windows, and turned the volume up. Strains of the first song filled the car. "Oh, lord. Junior year memories," Susan blurted out, fanning herself. The first time she noticed Tim as other than her school friend. More memories cropped up as she drove. The past had its place. Reminiscing worked fine their first night together. Time for a different conversation? She wasn't sure.

Susan turned down the volume as she approached the Emeryville exit. Twice during the drive, two of the songs tugged at her in ways they hadn't before. Lyrics about a heart learning to love again and taking risks on second chances opened her heart's floodgates. Several damp tissues lay in the trash bag between her and the passenger seat. She cared. No amount of denial could hide it. Moving back to Cascade Bay brought back memories good and bad, times of joy and sorrow, and ones of ultimate happiness like when she graduated in the upper third of her class. What did she do now? Risk again and take whatever happened as a life experience good or bad? Pulling up to a stoplight, she glanced in her rearview mirror. She smiled at her reflection, windblown hair, sunglasses partway down her nose, and a glow that made her wink at herself. Yes, she knew what her choices were. Planning mitigated some possibilities and brought others out in her forethoughts. Keeping aware and being open made the most sense.

The light changed. She popped out the CD once she was on the main road into Emeryville. The train station was on the opposite side of town. She glanced at the dashboard clock. Twenty minutes until the train arrived. She had time to pull through the fast-food drive-through two blocks from the station and grab a couple of ice-cream sodas for her and Tim. The park she passed on her way into town provided her the inspiration. They'd hung out in a park after school drinking homemade root beer floats and laughing while they talked. Maybe they could recapture that feeling. She hoped that opened the gate to the conversation she wanted to have with him.

Susan glanced toward the station doors as she pulled into the parking lot. No sign of Tim. The train sounded its horn announcing its arrival. She pulled into a parking space close to the front of the lot. She turned the ignition off and watched, noting every person who exited. Squinting, she shielded her eyes hoping to make out clearer any male who came out. Tim's height and hair color distinguished him from most other men. She fanned herself, thinking of how he looked during their morning together before he left.

Susan ran her fingers down the outside of the cup close to her collecting the moisture with her fingers. She trailed her fingers over her neck and down toward her cleavage. Cold drops of water trickled into her bra and down her neck. She sat upright as a breeze blew through the open window. She glanced down, ready to grab a napkin to blot any drops ready to wet her shirt.

"Hot enough for you?"

Susan shrieked, jumped, and pulled back her fist. She looked up. Tim stood outside the car, grinning. She scowled at him as he leaned down, lips puckered. "I shouldn't," she claimed before brushing her lips over his.

"Sorry. Didn't mean to startle you." Tim pulled back, walked around the car, and tried to open the passenger door. "Come on, hun. It's hot out here."

"Hmm, maybe I should?" Susan started the car, reached for the gearshift, and revved the motor.

"Please," Tim called out over the motor's noise. "I'm sorry."

Susan unlocked the doors. She waited until Tim tossed his case in the back and got in to voice her come back. "I didn't like it when you spooked me in school. Not in college either. Don't do it again, okay?"

Tim buckled his seat belt and faced her. He reached out toward her with his hand palm up. "I'm sorry. I won't do that again. Noted you don't like it."

Susan put the car in gear. She glanced at Tim. She pressed her lips together, hoping her merriment at his dejected look didn't escape her. Mary's statement about their connection being tenuous came roaring back. It felt solid the more she mulled it. They had a rusty link in their chain. One that could be broken or fixed to strengthen what they already restarted. Yes, that talk in the park made sense. She pulled out of the parking lot and turned toward the highway.

"Thank you," she began. "I think we need to talk. I found the perfect spot."

Tim rubbed his lips together, counting each breath. What was going on? His left palm itched. His right sweated. Taunts and coarse names rolled up in his conscience like a wildfire ready to burst out over the firewall in its path. He wiped his hand on his pants, scratched his other, and spoke. "All right. I hope things are okay."

Susan flicked the turn signal on. "For the most part. It's a few more minutes until we're there. One of the ice-cream sodas is for you. I got bottles of water, too."

"What flavor sodas did you get?" Tim picked up one of the cups examining the logo.

"Chocolate and strawberry. I remember you like both like I do." Susan pulled into the park's parking area. "Let's sit by the pond. It'll be cooler there."

Tim unfastened his seatbelt. He turned to Susan. "Before we do, may I say something?"

Susan reached for her purse, keys in hand. "Sure. Remember, I said talk. I'm not going to pick an argument."

Tim nodded. "Good. I was worried about that."

"Here." Susan pointed to the picnic tables near the pond. "We're away from home, business, and distractions. I put my cell phone on vibrate."

Tim pulled his out of his pocket. "I'm doing the same."

He opened his door and picked up the cup close to him. "Bottles of water?"

"In my tote. Come on. We've got these to enjoy." She held up the other cup. "Stop frowning. It's going to be fine."

Tim got out and made his way toward the table closest to the pond and still in the shade. He sat down facing the car. Susan followed, carrying the other cup and her tote. She sat down across from him.

"Have a straw." She took two out of her tote. "Take a few swallows and let go for a bit. Shift focus please."

Tim opened the straw, put it into his cup, and took a long draw. Chocolate mixed with mint flowed over his taste buds. Bits of chocolate chips followed the carbonation bubbling in his mouth. He looked at Susan who drank from hers. He waited until she set her cup down to speak. "Wow, that's good. This is from the place two blocks over from the station?"

"Yes. I saw the sign and remembered our homemade floats. Decided we deserved a treat." Susan leaned forward, laying her hands flat on the table.

"Thanks. I'll let you start the conversation." Tim drank more of his soda, savoring the sweet concoction.

"I think we're too caught up in the past." Susan took out a bottle of water and uncapped it. She drank and set the open bottle on the table next to her cup. "We spent the other night batting old incidents back and forth."

"True. We overcame that after a while." Tim raised his cup. "The evening turned out quite nicely."

Susan ducked her head. He could see the flush starting at her ears and traveling down her neck. So their night together and morning after affected her, too. Good, he started to breathe deeper. Now, if his stomach would spit out the butterflies and settle in one spot, he might enjoy his soda more.

"Yes, it did. The thing I'm wondering is can we move into the present. Enjoy our connection and see where it goes." Susan uncapped her soda cup, laying the lid on the table. She saluted him with her cup.

Was his mouth hanging open? His tongue hanging out? How much dismay showed on his face? Had she just propositioned him? He looked down, staring at the table in disbelief.

Ask her. You got a mouth. Ask and you'll know. What a time for the practical side of his conscience to show up!

Hey, if you listened to me more, you might not have made some of your mistakes.

"Shut up," Tim murmured. He winced at his sarcastic tone.

"What did you say?" Susan asked.

Tim looked up. Her intent gaze told him she'd caught part of what he said. "Ever talk to yourself?"

Susan cupped her chin, leaning on her elbow. She looked at him like he spoke a foreign language. Or blathered like his mind had jumped off the table and ran off without him.

"Seriously, I think out loud sometimes. *Too loudly.*" Tim shrugged and drank more of his soda.

Susan smiled, shaking her head. She winked as she pointed at him. "I'll go you one better. Lose an argument with yourself. Try explaining that one to your shrink."

"You, too? Told mine that I preferred acting out both roles to see both sides." Tim smirked.

"Okay, so our pasts messed with us. Had a few ready to stamp our records with indelible red ink." Susan snickered.

Tim laid his hand on the table close to Susan's. "This time I think we're able to call the shots ourselves."

"I agree. So you in?" Susan laid her hand on top of his.

Tim looked down again. He knew his heart cried out yes with each beat. His libido echoed the same. His ego laughed, cackling as his conscience tossed its opinion out again.

What about Karlene? You gotta tell her. Ain't right if you don't.

Tim pressed his lips together, forcing a smile he hoped shoved his blasted conscience's one-sided opinions back down its throat. He knew telling Susan mattered. And he would. Basking in the good feelings of their mutual desire to see more of each deserved a few more minutes before he busted that bubble wide open.

"Yes, I'm in." Tim raised their hands to his lips. He kissed each of Susan's knuckles, dragging his tongue along each finger until he reached the tip. He nibbled them slightly, turned her hand over, and pressed his lips to her palm. He closed her hand and spoke again. "I need to tell you something."

Susan's gaze met his. Her smile reached her eyes, making her glow in a way he hadn't seen since he asked her to the ninth-grade dance. Of course, acting like a bumbling teen male hadn't done that night any good. She blew him a kiss. He inhaled sharply. His next statement might smash the bubble beyond repair.

"What do you need to tell me?" Susan rubbed her cheek against his hand. She kissed the back of his hand and entwined her fingers with his.

Tim counted his breaths, willing his heart to slow its staccato beat. No matter how he said it or prefaced it, the words wouldn't change. He took one last breath and spoke. "I'm going to San Diego with Karlene for a week."

Chapter Nineteen

"You're what?" Susan yanked her hand away. "What the hell is going on?"

"Hold on." Tim leaned forward, reaching for her hand. She pulled back, rapidly sliding her arms off the table.

"No hold on. You..." Susan turned, straddling the bench. "You can't play with people's hearts."

Tim stood up. He rounded the table and dropped down on the bench next to her. "Play with your heart?"

"Damn it, yes," Susan spit out, wrapping her arms tightly around her. Every breath she took shook her deep into her aching ready-to-break heart. Why did she think he changed?

Tim kept waving his hand in front of her. He wanted her attention. He fucking had it and tossed it on the ground like a leaf. What next? Grind her under his thumb or heel deeper into the pit of despair ready to swallow her whole?

Susan slowly inhaled, forcing her shudders to slow. The deeper she inhaled, counting as she did, the more in control she got. Unwrapping her arms, she raised her head and glared at Tim.

Tim pressed his lips together. Susan's tight posture and dark scowl poured over him. Was it his tone? He hadn't hid what he said. Double crap and then some. It was like old times again...wait...was it? They were talking. Possibly fighting. They were communicating even if it was awkward. Maybe that was it. Yeah, it had to be. Susan wasn't stomping off. He wasn't stubbornly expecting her to come to him. This might work out. His next words could make or break both of their hearts.

Tim leaned forward. This time he wasn't taking no for an answer. "You can move back all you want. I need you to focus on what I'm saying. If you move, I follow."

Susan glared at him, shaking her head. So she had a stubborn side just like him. She could keep that defensive posture up all she liked. "You can say whatever you need to. I'm listening." Susan started to turn again.

"I need you to look at me. See me as I tell you what I need to say." He waited until her gaze met his. "I'm not playing with our hearts. My daughters need me."

Would Susan continue to listen?

"I'm not asking you to like this. I don't either. Jennifer and Hailey are screwing up big time. I've got to be there." Tim straddled the bench facing Susan. "Please tell me what you're feeling."

Susan's sniffle gut-punched him worse than if she'd told him to go fuck himself. Hurting someone he loved scorched him deep into his soul. If there was another way, he'd take it. Putting his kids first was going to happen from time to time. Could Susan accept this?

"I'm not sure how I feel." Susan's shuddered sigh said she might be thinking rather than reacting. Tim took a deeper breath. He motioned for her to continue.

"Maybe this is a part I hadn't considered yet. A missed piece of the puzzle." Susan reached for a napkin.

"I get it. I wish it hadn't happened so quickly. Karlene dropped the issue on me last night." Tim handed one of the napkins from the table to Susan. He spoke again. "My phone went dead before I could tell you."

"Sounds made up. You couldn't have called this morning?" Susan dabbed her eyes.

"I wanted to. Dickerson showed up with Stuart Churchwell at breakfast. Another meeting that neither Leslie nor I anticipated. State watchdog!" Tim laid his hand on the table close to Susan. "I'll tell you what's going on as we drive back, okay?"

He watched Susan take a deep breath. His id wanted him to glance down to where her chest rose and fell, to her bust and centering his thoughts on her breasts. Flexing his fingers, Tim kept his eyes on her face. Noting every blink, lip movement, and slight shoulder roll she made. He doubted she would leave him without a way back. Enduring an hour in silence might ache and gnaw deep into his heart and gut. He could withstand this. This might set back what they'd started. He wasn't giving up. Was she?

Susan held up two fingers, speaking. "Kids matter. You're showing me you care about yours."

He nodded. She folded one finger down. "We matter, too. I don't know where this is going. I'm not speculating." She laid her hand on top of his, smiled, and added, "I've got your back 'cuz we're friends."

Tim swallowed hard. *Friends.* That word could mean many different things and had so many levels. Nitpicking or trying to pinpoint anything accomplished nothing. San Diego, Karlene, and two in-deep-shit teens took priority tomorrow. Here and now mattered, and strengthening his connection with Susan topped his immediate to-do list.

"Thanks. Appreciate it." Tim laid his other hand on top of Susan's. "The explanation won't take long."

Susan pulled her hand out from under his. She slung her purse over her shoulder and reached for her tote. "It's okay if it does. Being a parent who cares matters. I want to know what's going on."

Tim looked down, blinked, and swallowed his response. Neither of them needed his sarcastic comeback or his quizzical curiosity taking over. "Okay," was all he dared say. Somehow this conversation, this moment—hell, all of it wasn't like any of their prior discussions.

Tim turned and found Susan staring at him. Lord, she watched him as intently as he did her. At least they'd broken the eggs, crushed the shells, and scrambled 'em good like his grandmother said when she tried to talk his teen angst out with him.

Tim stood, holding out his hand. "Sorry. Caught up in my thoughts. Makes me wonder if we put our parents through similar crap."

Susan took his hand, swinging one leg over the bench she sat on and then her other. She gripped his hand firmer as she stood. "Don't know how ours compares yet. I suspect all parents and kids have their *oh crap* moments. And a few *oh shit* ones, too."

Tim chuckled. "You may be on to something."

He walked to the trash receptacle close to them. Dropping in their cups and napkins, he glanced to where Susan stood. They'd gotten through an argument without either clamming up or walking away. Possibilities might be changing. He walked over to her, offered his hand, and nodded toward her car. "Shall we?"

"Sure," Susan said, taking his hand. Quietly they made their way to the car. Tim knew the next moments might be some growth-filled ones for them.

Ten more minutes passed without either of them talking. Susan glanced at Tim twice before she set the cruise control. Noting the mileage sign they passed a couple of moments prior, they had about fifty minutes until they reached the outskirts of Cascade Bay.

"What's going on with Karlene and the girls?" Susan took one hand off the steering wheel and laid it on Tim's arm. "It's gotta be big for you to need to go to San Diego."

Tim snorted, shook his head, and replied, "Big might be an understatement. Karlene and the girls moved to San Diego shortly after we divorced. About five years ago."

"Wow," Susan replied. "Talk about putting your past behind you."

"One of Karlene's sorority sisters lives there. She got her on with the company she worked for. Fresh start for them and a clean break for me. Sold the house and split the profits."

"Yes, you said your place was built after the divorce. How old are Jennifer and Hailey?" Susan put both hands on the steering wheel and clicked off the cruise control, stepping on the brake as traffic slowed in front of them.

"Jennifer is fifteen, thinking she's twenty-one. Hailey is thirteen and mimics her sister."

"Oh, the years when puberty really gets you knotted up." Susan turned on her blinker and changed lanes.

Tim pointed at the windshield. "Ahead of us, it looks like an accident with all the police cars and lights."

"Sure does. We're gonna have to take some back routes." Susan changed lanes again making her way across the highway toward the next exit.

"What are you thinking of for directions?"

"Something not across the bay bridges. Traffic will head there. Try San Rafael or Berkley. Once we're clear of the major congestion, I can stop to relocate us."

"Last sign did say exit forty-nine A for Berkley."

"Smart mouth. Go on with your story." Susan entered the exit lane, slowing down.

"The last couple of years, Jennifer started hanging out with a different group at school. Hailey tagged along. Their visits got fewer, too."

"You here. Them there. Not a lot you could do. "

"No. Karlene's cryptic conversations and texts left a lot unsaid, I'm finding out."

"How so?" Susan stopped at the bottom of the exit ramp. She looked both ways, noting where businesses or restaurants were.

Tim sighed. How did he admit he just figured this out after his last conversation with Karlene? Some father he turned out to be. Maybe more kids weren't a good idea. He licked his lips and replied, "Grade points dropping, trouble in school, and the busing issue. Gangs, too."

"OMG!" Susan gasped. "She didn't tell you this?"

"Apparently not in full. Some of it she alluded to or made light of. Guess she thought it was handled." He shook his head. His ex-wife wasn't handling her rude awakening very well from what he ascertained from her tone during their conversation.

Susan eased into traffic, turning to the left. Tim shifted in his seat so he could see her. "Let me say she has more silent conversations than speaking ones."

Susan's titter warmed him, easing a smile across his face. "I'm going to stop at the next restaurant. We can get better directions from the locals, I bet."

"Probably so. Let me say this about Karlene's and my discussion in short. We're pulling the girls out of school. With joint custody, I've got to be there, too." Tim noted the local fast-food chain and rubbed his hands. "Can we get sandwiches to go?"

Susan chortled. "Let's get some directions first. Then food, okay?"

"Yes, I'll get food scoped out. Bathroom, too." Tim unbuckled his seatbelt and reached for the door handle. "What would you like?"

"Chicken tenders and orange juice, please. In the glove box, there's a map book. Grab it." Susan pulled her purse onto her shoulder. She opened her door and got out.

Tim took the map book out of the glove box. He opened his door, grasping the book in his other hand. As he stepped out, his gaze met Susan's over the top of the car. She shot him a toothy grin and a wink then turned toward the restaurant. *Friends*, the word that kept them connected. However tenuous it seemed or felt, Tim knew his heart ached. He couldn't put words to it. Too soon too fast came to mind if he let his thought dwell on it. Right now wasn't the time to dissect. Moving forward mattered.

"Here's the map book. Bathroom first. Then food order." Tim handed Susan the map book and took off trotting toward the restaurant's door.

Ten minutes later, he stopped as he exited the men's room. Susan stood near the women's room door. She nodded, pushing the door open. He pointed toward the counter and moved into the dining area. The cashier walked over to the register as Tim approached. "Can I help you?"

"Yes," Tim began. "Order to go. Two chicken tender baskets. One orange juice and a lime sparkling water, please."

"Sauce choices?" The cashier entered his order up to that point.

Tim looked over his shoulder. Susan hadn't reappeared. She was in the restroom still. He looked at the sauces available, thought back to her recipe instructions, and smiled as he read the last sauce listed. "Chipotle barbecue, smoky southwest, and sweet-and-sour. Two of each, please."

"Total is ten seventy-two." The cashier placed the sauces on the counter. Tim handed her a twenty. He glanced over his shoulder again. Susan approached, her cell phone in hand.

"I checked with Nina. She and Leslie are about half an hour behind us. They stopped for lunch. Local radio station says to take the inland freeway and double back." Susan slipped her phone into her purse.

"Did you get directions?" Tim accepted his change from the cashier.

"Yes, it's going to take us back the way we came for a distance, then on to the inland freeway that will get us to Berkeley about four." Susan took the orange juice bottle he held out to her.

Tim looked at his watch. "It's two fifteen now. That isn't too bad."

"Hope you don't have to be somewhere soon." Susan pointed at the counter. "Order's ready."

He picked up the bag and bottle of sparkling water that sat on the counter. "Thank you. Have a good day."

"Same to you, sir. Safe drive," the cashier responded.

Back out in the car, Susan faced him. She held the GPS. "This shows us going the same way we were."

"Ain't doing that. How far do we backtrack?" Tim opened his bottle.

"Five miles and then take exit forty-four B toward Napa then head south toward State Route three fifty-eight." Susan started the car. "There's a cup holder in the console between us. Lever on your side opens it."

Tim opened the console, setting their drinks and bag of food inside. "I dumped the fries and tenders together."

"Okay. You got the chipotle sauce. It's good. Open one and we'll dunk as we can." Susan backed out of the parking space and headed toward the exit.

"Here's to the drive home." She saluted him with a tender.

Tim raised his. "Salute."

Fifteen minutes passed until they were back on the highway going back the direction they'd come. Susan shook her head as they passed a long line of cars on the opposite side of the highway. "Yikes. They are going to be there a while. Manager said a four-car pileup with multiple injuries occurred between their exit and the next five miles up. Emergency response has both sides blocked off."

"Glad we aren't sitting there." Tim sipped his water. "You got questions for me on what's going on with Karlene?"

"How you going to handle this?" Susan glanced at him.

"Not sure beyond signing them out of school. Don't know what plans Karlene has." Tim laid his hand on Susan's arm. "Another reason this trip with her is important."

Susan moved her arm away, putting both hands on the wheel. "Doesn't sound like you two communicate well. I'm wondering if you need time to get this ironed out."

"We probably do. That's why I texted her about flying down together from San Francisco."

Susan glanced at him, frowning. "Okay."

Tim grimaced. There was no mistaking the iciness layering between them. He pressed his lips together and exhaled. How did he explain this? He rolled his shoulders and spoke, "This isn't easy for either of us. I appreciate you hearing me out. Strategize with me?"

"For what? Help you circumvent your ex? Doesn't sound like something I want any part of." Susan didn't look at him or move beyond driving. Yet her tone, acidic and dripping with ire, flipped him her middle finger as clearly as if she'd gone ahead and done so.

Tim slipped his tongue between his teeth, clenching his other hand in a tight fist. Who pushed his buttons more? His tight-lipped ex-wife or his potential sitting across from him. Leslie hadn't helped either when he learned what Karlene said and the plan Tim had to head her off. Leslie wished him well, adding bringing Susan into the mix might set off more than he anticipated. Looked like Leslie garnered points there. Overall score was Tim triple zip and everyone else playing by their rules. *Unspoken ones, too.* "I'm *not* circumventing anyone. I want what's best for my kids. How I go about that is a jumbled mess thanks to my ex. Seems no one wants to help either."

"Asking me to help you strategize puts me in the middle, doesn't it?" Susan plucked a french fry out of the bag and popped it in her mouth. She changed lanes, moving them toward the merger with state route three fifty-eight.

"No. It doesn't." Tim held up his hand as Susan opened her mouth to reply. "Let me clarify. I bounce ideas off you. You respond with questions and your reactions."

"That's what I've been doing. I really think this is your problem. Not mine to get into." Susan picked up her juice, holding the bottle out to him. "It's like me asking you to open this again. It already is. Or hand me food when I can get it."

Tim slumped in his seat. "There's no easy way to this."

Susan shot him a glare and responded, "No, there isn't. So what are you going to do?"

Tim uncapped his drink, took a swig, and set the bottle down. He swallowed, then replied, "Talk with Karlene and see what we can work out."

"Won't be easy, I'm sure. What can I do to help otherwise?" Susan laid her hand on his.

Tim took a deep breath and asked, "Spend the night and part of tomorrow with me in San Francisco?"

Chapter Twenty

Two Days Later

"Why didn't you go?" Nina picked up her burger and bit into it. She rolled her eyes upward. She chewed watching Susan toy with her chef's salad, one of Jeff's specialties.

Nina wiped her mouth and spoke again. "Something wrong with your salad? Jeff will want to know." She started to raise her hand. Susan looked up, pointing her fork at her.

"Nothing's wrong with the salad. Stop poking already, okay?" Susan forked some of the salad into her mouth.

Nina rocked back in her chair, tossed her napkin on the table, and sounded off. "You're the one whose attitude is hanging out. Don't grumble at me."

Susan shrugged and continued eating. Nina tucked her napkin back on her lap and continued eating

Moments of silence passed. Each of them ate while occasionally eyeing the other.

Off to the side, Jeff stood behind the counter, watching the antics of the two. He picked up his cell phone off the counter, thumbing through his contacts. Finding the one he sought, he pressed dial and walked into the kitchen out of earshot of the diners. On the third ring, Mary answered.

"Jeff, what's up?" Mary asked.

"Got a question for you."

"Okay."

"What's with Susan and Nina?" Jeff pulled the chair out from his desk, sitting down.

"Why do you ask?"

"She and Nina are bristling at each other." Jeff held the phone away from his ear, waiting for Mary's lecture on his eavesdropping.

"You can put the phone back to your ear." Mary paused as if she were waiting for him to do this and tell her he had.

Jeff smiled and put the phone on speaker, laying it on his desk. "Speaker is better."

With Nina and Leslie's wedding less than a week and a half off, he needed both of his business partners focused on the last-minute preparations. He hadn't signed on for refereeing arguments.

Mary sighed. "I'm making my way back to the shop. I'll drop by your delivery door. Let me in and I'll explain."

Mary hung up before he could say yes or no. Jeff pushed back from his desk and stood. He quickly made his way to the delivery door. As he swung it open, Mary trotted into sight. "Hi," she said, stopping as she reached the top step. "Good weather for a run."

Jeff nodded, holding the door open. "Come in. I'll get us a couple of bottles of water. Go on in the office."

Mary nodded and slipped into the short hall leading to his office. Jeff quickly made his way to the front where he snagged two bottles of water from the cold case behind the lunch counter. Susan and Nina sat quietly, still consuming their lunch. He shook his head. Susan and Nina needed an intervention. How did he and Mary accomplish that without setting off more fireworks?

"Angela, keep an eye on table four, please. If they leave, let me know." He and Mary needed a swift actionable plan.

"You got it," Angela replied.

Jeff closed his office door as he entered. He handed Mary a bottle of water. She sat in the chair in front of his desk. In front of her sat a plate with mixed fruit pieces.

"Okay, Nina and Susan are still sulking. Angela is keeping an eye on them." Jeff slid into the chair behind his desk.

"Good. What I say is between us. Got it?" Mary uncapped her bottle and drank. She popped a couple of grapes into her mouth and chewed, waiting for Jeff's answer.

"Yes. Go ahead."

"Susan's sweet on Tim. Kinda dating him." Mary picked up a grape and bit into it.

"Tim, the best man?" Jeff whistled lowly.

Mary swallowed, wiped her mouth, and replied, "The same. They've got history. Not a great one either."

"Sounds chancy if you ask me." Jeff drank part of his water, reaching for one of the apple chunks on Mary's plate.

"Take two—I'm not going to finish all of this." Mary pushed the plate between them. "Susan confided in me that she cares for Tim a lot."

"Where does Nina come in?" Jeff bit into the chunk of apple, savoring its tart sweetness and crunch.

"She and Susan haven't talked about Susan's feelings." Mary took a piece of cantaloupe, raising it toward her mouth. "I think they snuck up on her."

"You know this and Nina doesn't." Jeff bit into the rest of the apple chunk. Gods above, what did he and Mary do now? How deep was she involved?

"Right. Did you hear any of their conversation?" Mary bit into the piece of cantaloupe.

Did this require all three women talking? How to keep any of them from feeling like they were in the middle was beyond him. He washed the rest of the apple down with another hefty swig of water. Taking a deep breath, he leaned back in his chair, holding up his hand. "I caught bits and pieces as I delivered their order. Trip, Tim, and kids came up. Their silence in between long stares followed."

"Sounds like—" A hard knock on the office door sounded cutting Mary off. Jeff rose, calling out as he did, "Yes."

Angela opened the door. "I checked on them. They're almost done eating. I mentioned dessert."

"Thanks, Angela, I'll be out in a moment." Jeff waited until the door closed before he said more. He took a deep breath, nodded, and tossed his idea on the table. "What about you join them for dessert?"

Mary shrugged, standing up. "You go out first. They know I come to see you from time to time. I can follow."

"Let's see if we can get them talking." Jeff opened the door, glancing at Mary as he did. "Nina and Leslie's wedding is less than ten days away. I'd like it to go off without a hitch."

Angela hovered near the dining room entrance holding two menus. "I'll take care of this," Jeff said, reaching for the menus. "Thanks, Angela."

Jeff moved to the table, Mary at his side. He laid the menus on the table.

Susan looked up first. "Hi, Mary."

Nina turned, smiling. "Mary, nice to see you."

Mary moved into his line of vision, pulling a chair with her. "Jeff said you were here. I could use some ice tea and one of Jeff's cream cheese pastries. May I join you?"

Nina spoke up first. "Sure. I think I'd like one of those, too. And some coffee."

Susan glanced at her watch. "Our four o'clock with the Murphys?"

"Taken care of. They came in. Paid their deposit. Left a check for their reception catering and approved the menu. I'll bring them over to Jeff on my way home." Mary sat down handing the menus to Jeff. "You gotta try these cream cheese croissants. They're delicious."

"Sounds good. Decaf tea please." Susan glanced at Jeff, catching his nod before he walked away. She waited until Jeff was out of sight before turning back to Nina and Mary. "How much did he hear?"

Mary frowned. Susan folded her hands together and leaned on them, resting her elbows on the table. She glanced at Nina who toyed with the lettuce from her burger. Mary kept looking forward like she avoided making eye contact. Susan steepled her index fingers, tapping them against her chin, she asked, "Do I have to ask again?"

Mary turned in her chair. "No. He heard some. Enough to ask me what was going on."

"Great. My business partner eavesdrops on my conversations." Susan crumpled the napkin lying on the table next to her. She stared at Mary, adding, "And my other..."

Mary laid her hands on the table and bent forward. "I asked him what he heard. What bothered him. You and Nina don't fight."

Nina snorted and burst out laughing. "Oh, we fight. Some humdingers from time to time. We don't let it ruin our friendship."

"So you tell each other everything?" Mary tilted back in her chair.

Susan looked down. She'd told Nina a bit about her interest in Tim and his asking her to go to San Francisco with him. Mary only knew how strong her attraction to Tim was and that she'd gone out with him. Nina didn't know she'd spent the night with him or the morning after. No, that was between her and

Tim. Mary picked up on the unsaid portion of their conversation, stating that what Susan did on her time wasn't anyone else's business.

"Umm," Nina began. Susan looked up, noting Mary watched Nina. "Most everything," Nina continued.

"What's ours to tell. Right, Nina?" Susan picked up her glass, stirred the ice with her straw, and sucked water through the straw.

"Pretty much," Nina said, nodding her agreement.

Susan looked at Mary. Was she going to share what she knew? Susan hoped not. Mary had gotten the part about the unsaid portion of what she heard. Even though neither of them had said the word sex or overnight when they talked. Nina's already short fuse would go off again if she found out from Mary about her overnight with Tim. Nina had enough on her mind.

"Good. I like my friends comfortable knowing that they may not know everything." Mary leaned back as Jeff approached carrying a tray. Angela followed with another laden with their drinks. Quiet ensued until Jeff and Angela left.

Susan blew on her tea before sipping. Nina's arched brow and sideways glance reached across the table without any effort. Susan knew that look. Nina gave that glance when she worked hard to keep her retort to herself. Susan sipped more tea, clutching the mug tighter than she liked. Spilling all didn't feel right. Was there a way to get Mary and Nina's help without doing that?

"I value privacy and want my friends to do the same. Know they don't have to tell me everything." Susan sat her mug down.

Nina picked up her pastry and turned it left and right as if she examined it very carefully. She set the pastry down and pointed at Mary. "I don't know what you know. You don't know what I know. Maybe that is where it needs to be."

Susan dropped her hand into her lap, wiping her sweaty palm across her napkin. She had to say something or the snarky stabs would grow. She inhaled, wet her lips, and jumped into the abyss called telling the truth. Crossing her fingers—and her ankles—crap, the fingers on her other hand, too, which also lay in her lap, she'd cross her legs except that would knock the table and possibly kick Mary and Nina. Talk about knotting your own bloomers and she didn't own such a garment resembling those. Well, it would take much more to knot her panties. Susan ducked her head, hoping neither Mary nor Nina caught her blushing at her own pun and innuendo. Both would want to know why her neck and cheeks flushed.

She raised her head and observed Mary and Nina watching each other. Damn, this was like two cats waiting for the other to hiss or spit first. Neither would make a scene here. Mary would keep her cool no matter what. She didn't let much break her peace. That's what drew Susan to her when she began looking for a florist to team up with. Nina would sputter a bit then blow when they were one-on-one later.

"Okay," Susan said, gulping air as Mary and Nina looked at her. "Tim and I...we've been kind of dating."

Mary pulled back, puzzlement written all over her face. Nina looked away and back, arching her brows even more.

"Kinda?" Nina asked, sarcasm dripping off her voice leaving no doubt she wasn't buying what she heard.

"I agree with her." Mary pointed at Nina.

Susan tried to inhale deeper than her last breath. Wasn't happening. "I—hic—I—" Another hiccup followed by another sounded. Susan grabbed her near-empty water glass and swallowed the bits of ice and fluid remaining. Water coated her dry throat, calming the next hiccup threatening to escape. "I told the truth."

"Yeah, right," Nina tossed back, her voice colder than before.

Susan exhaled, rolling her shoulders. How much more did she reveal? Tell and share without pushing Tim and her under anyone's bus.

Mary tapped on the table, getting Susan and Nina's attention away from their smoking angst. She held up her pastry. "Like the pastry each of us has, we've got layers. Some flake off and show who we are underneath."

Susan and Nina nodded. Good, they followed her train of thought. Mary continued her train of thought. "What's inside we know because we created the inside together. Well, Jeff did, and we trust he delivered what we asked for."

"True. So you're saying trusting each other is important." Susan bit into her pastry.

"Vital to me," Nina stated, holding her pastry aloft. "An important part of my core group. Those in it I trust implicitly."

"Okay," Mary said. "Then we need to be honest and upfront with each other, right?"

Susan and Nina nodded again.

"I think Susan is telling us what she can. I trust she'll share what is important and hers to tell." Mary held up her glass of ice tea. "Here's to hearing Susan out."

Nina wiped her mouth, raised her mug. "Yes and trusting what she tells us."

"Thanks," Susan said, holding her mug up. "Let me get us all on the same page."

Clinking of china and glass sounded. Susan retold of running into Tim at the grocery store, their meal together, and helping with transportation to and from the train station. While she spoke, Mary and Nina enjoyed their pastries and drinks. Susan broke off pieces of hers, nibbling on them when she paused. She sipped her tea while Mary and Nina ate the last of their pastries.

Nina wiped her mouth. She laid the napkin on top of her plate. "Did you tell Mary about yours and Tim's past?"

Before Susan could answer, Mary spoke. "Yes, that is one area we discussed a lot."

Susan opened her mouth again. Nina held up her hand. "Mary and I got this. Why a lot?"

Mary glanced at Susan, then back to Nina, and answered. "Because it's the past. And being bogged down by it. Not seeing the here and now."

"Like not letting go? Or learning from it?" Nina swallowed more coffee.

Mary barely opened her mouth when Susan blurted out, "Damn straight. Tim got hung up on apologizing for what he considered past mistakes. I keep waiting for him to be different."

Nina faced her. Her gaze looked past her like she wasn't there. More in thought and processing the ideas pulsing through her psyche. Nina parted her lips, shook her head, and closed her mouth. She blinked and glanced at Mary, nodding as she did. Nina wet the tip of one finger and dragged it through the air five times. She offered Mary a high five next.

Susan squinted, blinked, and glimpsed at Mary. She sat still, both hands holding her ice tea glass. Nina started to lower her palm. Mary set the glass down and leaned forward, hand up to Nina. As Mary's palm touched Nina's, Nina pointed at Susan with her other hand. "I owe you an apology. "

"No, you don't," Susan said, vigorously shaking her head.

"Hush," Nina uttered. "I do because I kept waiting for you or Tim to mess up like you used to do. Didn't see you as you are now. "

"Exactly what all of us do. Our minds speak from experience and we act on what we know." Mary held out her hand to Susan, her other hand palm to palm with Nina's. "Together we can work on being here and now."

Susan laid her palm against Mary's. She laid her free hand palm up on the table, speaking as she did. "I value both your friendships. I've got to let go of the past, too. We all do."

"How does this relate to you and Tim?" Nina looked from her to Mary and back.

"Tim is dealing with Karlene and his kids right now. He's got to decide is he going to keep looking back or move into the here and now."

Mary lowered her hand to the table. "What you're saying is creating a future together requires both of you be present here, knowing the past is done."

Nina nodded. "I get it. Leslie and I had to work through similar things. We had to decide where we started and others stopped."

"No more fixing the past. Work on now envisioning and building the future you want." Susan dropped her hands to the table. "If I went with Tim, his attention would be split."

Mary pushed back from the table. "Sounds to me like Tim is facing the part of being a dad and having a new relationship at the same time."

Nina chuckled and stood. "Leslie said Tim called yesterday, saying he needed an interpreter between Karlene's short sentences and his acronym-speaking daughters."

Jeff watched as the three women embraced. He smiled as he headed into his office. Now maybe he could focus on attentively getting the final touches done for Nina and Leslie's wedding.

Chapter Twenty-One

Three Days Later

"You're coming back already?" Leslie reached for his day planner. Forms and other papers lay scattered across his desktop.

"Karlene made up her mind before we came down. She's moving back." Tim's frustration came through loud and clear. His even flat tone followed by, "What a mess," said it all.

Leslie looked at his watch and checked his schedule. He could get to San Francisco by four. "What time does your flight get in?"

"Took the train. I've got Jennifer and Hailey with me." Tim's voice muffled. A few words came through. "No, you can't use my phone. Mom has both of yours."

Leslie caught his tongue between his teeth. One of the girls had a vocabulary full of cuss words she tossed at Tim.

"Jennifer, go back to your seat and keep your mouth shut." Tim's firmer, deeper voice said what hat he wore—a parent dealing with a pushing the limits kid.

"Hey," Leslie said, hoping to get Tim's attention. "What station? I'll meet you."

"San Jose. Thanks—could use the help. Karlene's brother Bob and his wife are taking the girls." Tim's pitch picked up.

"What time?" Leslie turned to the afternoon portion of the day's page.

"Six. Synced with Bob taking the girls camping with him and his family. A week backpacking away from the city." Tim's enthusiastic tone sent shivers across Leslie's shoulders. And Nina wanted kids right away? Somehow waiting a while looked so much better at the moment.

"Okay. Pick you up at six. Got it. See you then." Leslie scribbled the entry in his planner. He slid it to the side. He reached for the sheets he'd been reading when Tim's call came in. Figures and statistics combined with the state's request for detailed preliminary reports took more attention than he had. Picking up the blue highlighter close to him, Leslie started highlighting columns and numbers he needed. He didn't envy Tim. Figures and spreadsheets didn't talk back like kids could or did.

Tim shoved his cell phone deep into his jeans pocket. Twice Jennifer had tried tricking him into giving up his phone. Hailey sulked, barely speaking to him civilly since they changed from the train's through bus to the next train. Flying would have gotten them north quicker. Avoiding run-ins with any problems or slack in control made the train more efficient. Jennifer kept claiming her boyfriend was coming for her. Hailey echoed the sentiment until he asked about where their friends were as they made their last connection in Santa Barbara. Jennifer finally changed her whine when Tim showed her the reports Karlene e-mailed about the teens' vagrancy pick up by the San Diego police and the teens' release to border patrol agents due to their illegal status and outstanding warrants across the border. Three more hours until Bob took Jennifer and Hailey off his hands. Keeping the girls busy while Karlene finished up with the movers in San Diego took more focus than Tim realized. Being a parent wasn't easy nor was this going to get any easier. It was time for him to take on the "involved father" role again. Prepared or not, he wasn't backing away. Even Karlene admitted she needed his help. It would take a staunch approach and attentive concentration by him and Karlene. Great, where did that leave him and Susan? Her hands-off response to his request for help brainstorming had him back where he started, trying to start a new relationship and being a dad simultaneously. "And split yourself in two," he muttered, making his way back through the train coach noting where Jennifer and Hailey were. Slumped down in their seats, arms folded tight across their chests, glaring at each other from time to time and out the window.

Wrappers from their lunch littered the table between Jennifer and Hailey. Their appetites didn't wane regardless of their lament they weren't hungry. Good thing Karlene had warned him about blackmail attempts with refusing to eat. Tim shoved his hands into his pockets. Rubbing his hands together gleefully didn't come across as dad-like, though he wanted to puncture the balloons of guilt Jennifer and Hailey thought they had surrounding them. Guilt they thought they projected outward. Now he understood why Karlene said he had a lot of shit to shovel through to regain his parental footing with the girls. Karlene's sigh after she'd talked to the girls before leaving San Francisco told him she hadn't fared better in many areas. Teens full of angst, moodiness, and sure they knew best for themselves and everyone else. Had he and his siblings put his parents through similar shit?

Tim took one step into the set of facing seats area and cleared his throat. "Jennifer, sit up please. Hailey, you, too. We need to talk." He sat down in the seat closest to the aisle blocking the exit from the seats.

Jennifer muttered, shaking her head trying to turn farther from him. Hailey turned her head away from him. Tim reached out, grabbed part of the wrappers on the table, crinkling them as he spoke, distinctly enunciating each word. "Your temper tantrums are over. *Finished right now.*"

"Says who?" Jennifer tossed at him, sticking her tongue out before looking away.

"I do. Your father." Tim leaned forward, tossing the crumpled wrappers in Jennifer's lap.

She looked up, grabbing them, ready to fling them back at him. Tim placed both hands on the table, shaking his head emphatically. Hailey opened her mouth, ready to spew forth some nonsense he was sure. He raised one hand, snapped his fingers, and spoke again. "Stop acting like two-year-olds, both of you. If you want to be treated like fifteen- and thirteen-year-olds, then show some maturity."

Hailey snapped her mouth shut. Her cheeks coloring as she ducked her head. Good, he caught her where she lived, trying to be a teenager rather than a tween as Jennifer kept referring to herself. Jennifer sat upright in her seat, opening her fist and dropping the papers she held on the table. She picked up the bag next to her and began stuffing wrappers and loose paper into it. Tim caught her glances at him every time she put something in the bag.

"It's going in the trash. *Nowhere* else." Tim held his hand out for the bag. "Come on. I promised chocolate milkshakes. The café car has them."

Jennifer stood up, slinging her messenger bag over her shoulder. Hailey latched her fanny pack around her waist, a small smile beginning at the mention of chocolate. Jennifer led the way from their coach through the next coach until they reached the café car. Along the way, Tim noted where she glanced and her gaze lingered. His daughter had a thing for good-looking young men. What else made them up, neither of them knew. He knew one thing. His daughters weren't youngsters anymore. Even Hailey smiled, speaking to a young man who brushed passed her. Two young women moved ahead of him. Reconnecting with his daughters was going to take time and energy. Both of which he would need plenty of.

Tim sat in the booth closest to the counter, pointing to the seats across from him. "All right. I'm ready to dive into some chocolate. What about you guys?"

"Yeah, sure." Jennifer's lackluster response covered most of her conversations. Karlene mentioned this in her briefing on the flight to San Diego. He turned to Hailey, who licked her lips as she trailed her finger down the menu on the table.

"Dad, can I have a double chocolate soda instead?" Her eyes lit up as her gaze met his. "With chocolate sprinkles, too? Please."

Tim smiled. "Sure. You like chocolate like I do."

Hailey nodded vigorously. His baby—well, his youngest—didn't seem to be down on him as much as her sister. He turned to Jennifer. She looked down apparently at the menu as well.

"What has your attention?" Tim asked, leaning forward. "I think a shot of peppermint might add zing to my malt."

"Might," Jennifer offered, glancing at him.

Tim laid his hand on the table, palm up. "Look, I know this isn't easy."

"You could've been a better dad." Jennifer glanced away again. Then back at him. "Well, you could have."

Tim inhaled. Jennifer started the conversation. His reply could make or break the conversation moving forward. "Possibly. Yes, I could have. What do you think would've done that?"

Jennifer rattled off a list of things. Tears leaked out of her eyes. Hailey tossed in an item or two until Tim held his hands up. "Okay, I get you resent I wasn't around. Right now I want to get our order placed. Then discuss this more."

He rose and moved to the counter placing their orders. Ten minutes passed with quiet building between them. He turned back to the table, carrying their drinks. As he set them on the table, he spoke. "Jennifer, I wanted to be there for you. You, too, Hailey. Traveling to San Diego isn't cheap. I work, too."

Hailey reached for the second glass, tapping her paper-wrapped straw on the table. "Couldn't you have come for some stuff?"

"Communication goes both ways. I could have called more. You could have said what you wanted me at." Tim slipped his straw into his milkshake and sucked up a long swallow. He glanced at Jennifer. She toyed with her straw, stirring her drink. "What else you got to say, Jennifer?"

"Dad, you let us down." She started drinking her malt.

"Maybe we let each other down?" Tim picked up the spoon lying next to him. He stirred his milkshake. He looked at Hailey, who watched him intently. Jennifer opened her mouth, shut it, and shook her head.

Tim laid his hand on Jennifer's. "Responsibility isn't always easy. For now, let's work on rebuilding our relationship."

Hailey shrugged, drinking more of her soda. Jennifer's brief nod said she heard him. Reconnecting with his daughters mattered. Getting them talking helped. Tim glanced at his watch. Two more hours until Bob took over. Karlene left it in his hands to keep the girls in line. They choose the trip. At least that's what Karlene said.

"Are you ready for this hike?" Tim bit his lip, catching Hailey's gloat as her head tipped back. Jennifer nudged her sister.

"Mom said we had two choices, either help her or go with Uncle Bob. Freedom is precious. Under Mom's thumb, no thanks." Jennifer gulped more of her malt.

Hailey nodded. "Mom's been a real tyrant lately."

Tim looked down, pressing his lips together. Maybe the four of them needed an intervention. One from someone not so close to things. Sessions with a good shrink might do them all good. One thing at a time for now.

"Her side of it says you both weren't stellar either. Sounds like it needed to come to a halt." Tim finished his milkshake. He pushed his glass aside. "Freedom is earned, Jennifer. Uncle Bob isn't a pushover. You mess up, and he's going to come down hard, too. Same for you, Hailey."

Both girls nodded. Finishing their drinks, they stood up. "Can we go back to our seats? The kids near us said we could play one of their games." Hailey jiggled from one foot to another.

Tim sighed, nodded, and rose. They'd made some headway. He'd take that for now. More head butts would certainly follow once Hailey and Jennifer found out about private school and their restricted freedom come September.

Chapter Twenty-Two

Tim followed the girls back to their seats. A group of similar-aged kids invited them to join the board game they were starting. He settled back in his seat, sitting such that he could see the group easily. He pulled out his cell phone and scrolled through his text messages. One from Karlene caught his eye. The movers would leave out in two days with the furniture. She was at her sorority sister's until the next day. Good, having the house ready when the girls got back would help settle them in. Leslie's text was next. It read, "Sorry. Can't pick you up. Stuart's in town and wants info for state tonight."

"Great," Tim groaned. "Who's picking me up then?" His phone buzzed rousing him from his self-pity bent. He glanced down, rolled his eyes, and wondered if the powers-that-be had him on their sarcastic humor list. Susan's message read, "I'm picking you up. Got my battle gear with me. How loaded for barbs and loathes should I be?"

Resisting the urge to click his phone off, Tim placed it back in his pocket. He rose, made his way over to where the game went. One of the teens looked up and asked if he wanted to join them. He nodded and slid into the empty seat next to Jennifer. She slid him the rulebook as the others started setting up the game. Losing himself in the opposite direction for the next two hours made a lot of sense. He'd deal with putting his own battle armor on once they reached San Jose.

Susan pulled into the train station parking lot. As she pulled in, she didn't see Tim. Tim's short text didn't provide descriptions of Hailey and Jennifer. All she could do was sit and wait. The dashboard clock showed fifteen minutes until the train's scheduled arrival. Parking close to the front of the lot, her car stood out. Tim couldn't miss it. She hoped he didn't. Making nice with two brooding teens ran outside her experience. Mary and Nina's suggestion of trying what their parents tried with them was outmoded and like a thin sheet of ice cracking. Wouldn't work. She took a deep breath and let go a long sigh, counting slowly to fifteen. If she and Tim were going to move forward on their connection and renewed interest, she'd have to figure out how to communicate with the girls. Susan closed her eyes and replayed her list of topics her cousin's daughter gave her for discussion starters.

First was sports—professional or school level. What ones did Jennifer or Hailey play? Interests? Two— A rap sounded on the window. Susan jumped, yelling. "What the fuck!"

She pulled back her fist, turned in her seat, and started laughing. Tim stood outside the car, making inane faces at her. No one else stood near him. She rolled down the window. He leaned in, lips puckered, trying to whisper. "Wiss me. Beals are witching."

"What?" Susan pulled back. "What the hell did you say?"

Tim unpuckered as he got closer. "Kiss me. The girls are watching. They know a girlfriend is picking me up."

Susan shrugged and brushed her lips over Tim's. Claimed her as his girlfriend already? They hadn't had that talk yet. He needed a reality check if he thought things happened that easily. "Okay, you got your kiss," Susan said, pulling back. "Where are the girls?"

"Two rows over getting into their uncle's van. Karlene's brother has them for the week." Tim winked and pulled back. He leaned down, picked up his suitcase, and walked around the car.

As Tim opened the back passenger door, Susan noted the van pulling out two rows over with a window open and a youth flipping the bird in their direction. Great, a reputation with his kids already and without an introduction either. This didn't bode well for the discussion she and Tim needed to have. She started the car, glanced at Tim, and licked her lips. Susan put the car into gear, wondering how to initiate the discussion.

The click of Tim fastening his seatbelt cut through the quiet filling the space between them. Susan pointed to the map the GPS displayed. "We've got forty minutes until we get to the highway. You need anything?"

Tim yawned, shaking his head. "No thanks. Got a bottle of water. I need sleep."

Susan exited the parking lot before she glanced Tim's way again. His soft snores told her he had checked into slumberland without waiting for her reply.

At the next stoplight, she reached over, pulled his water bottle free from his hand, and placed it in the console's cup holder. Tim's snores quieted the closer to the freeway on-ramp she got. According to the GPS, the trip to Cascade Bay would take two hours with current traffic and time of day.

Susan moved toward the closest exit for Hayward ninety minutes later. Two miles down the main road into town, she pulled into the diner's parking lot. She glanced at Tim who dozed. His chest rose and fell with a rhythmic pattern. He slept deeply. The two-hour drive from San Jose was turning into a three-hour-plus drive thanks to midweek traffic and several accidents.

Rather than pushing through, stopping made sense. Taking time to discuss what came next plucked at her from the moment she'd kissed him. So much had happened and on the fly in some instances. Letting go of their past meant starting over with an outlook that kept the present in front of them. Could they move beyond what brought them to who they were now? Forgiving each other mattered. Making lists and checking them off wouldn't work either. Different things signified moments in their lives that influenced who they were now. So how did they leave the past where it belonged and move into a future built together? Nina's parting question echoed deep in her psyche. Had they forgiven themselves? Embraced their history and meshed it with the here and now they had? Susan liked to think she had. Maybe her actions said otherwise. Crap, where did they start then? Anywhere is where they started. No more avoiding the elephant in the backseat. The future mattered.

"Tim," Susan said, reaching over and laying her hand on his shoulder. She rubbed. Tim moved some. He blinked and zonked out again. She gripped his shoulder and shook. "Come on. Wake up." Susan shook him again.

Tim yawned and sat up. "What's wrong?"

"Traffic and accidents. It's after seven. I'm hungry." Susan unfastened her seatbelt.

Tim glanced at his watch. He muffled another yawn. Combing his hand through his hair, he replied, "I could eat, too."

Susan waited until they sat down and they ordered before she spoke again. "Have you thought about us?"

Tim set his water glass down. He arched an eyebrow, squinting as he looked at Susan. "What do you mean?"

"A lot has happened. We connect. Reminisce. The chemistry ensues. Then your ex and kids plunge in." Susan sipped her water.

He took a drink, inhaled, and pressed his lips together. She wanted an answer. Had he thought about them? Good god, yes. The night together. Their drives to and from Emeryville. All of it wasn't far from his thoughts even among his parenting moments. There was one answer. "Yes, I thought about us."

"Did you think about here and now, the present? Or are you stuck in the past? Still wanting to apologize?" Susan spread her napkin across her lap.

Tim swallowed hard, pressing his lips tighter together this time to keep his retort constrained. Talk about a one-two punch. What brought this about? Unwrapping his utensils, he unfolded his napkin. He didn't look up or down, only at the plain white paper napkin before him. Could he answer and not create more waves? Fuck, did anything he said or did not make waves? Licking his lips, he raised his gaze to Susan's, nodded, and saluted her with his glass. Watching the puzzlement wash over her, he gave himself an internal thumbs up. Catching her off guard might work in his favor if they were arguing. Susan's calm tone said anger didn't color her conversation or thoughts. So what did she want? Why was she asking these direct questions?

"I–I..." Susan stuttered like he demanded an answer. Shit, were his emotions that clear? His face showed what his psyche refused to voice, dismay, anxiety, and a dose of fear? Christ, he hoped not.

"Stop," Tim interrupted. "I'm not asking for rationale. I thought about us. I feel a need to apologize. My kids are great at pushing my guilt buttons."

"And us?" Susan stated, holding up her hand. "One thing at a time."

Tim nodded. "Guilt runs deep in some areas. I think men tend to feel it differently depending on the people and situation. With us, over missed chances and dumb shit, sure."

"Me, too," Susan threw out.

"Y–you do?" Tim reached up, capturing his chin with his hand. Okay, his mouth wasn't hanging open too far. Caught off guard seemed to be the style for this discussion.

"Yes. Until I realized something." Susan didn't say more. He looked to where she pointed. Their server approached the table with their order.

Five minutes' worth of silence pooled between them. Platters of hot steaming food sat before them. Susan moved the condiment tray closer to them. She stirred her mashed potatoes and gravy together and cut into a slice of meatloaf. She looked up, saluted him with her fork, and started eating.

He added pepper and some hot sauce to his shrimp fettuccine alfredo. He dumped parmesan cheese on top of the noodle mix and stirred. He saluted Susan in a similar style with a fork full of pasta. Neither of them spoke until several bites of food passed their lips.

"What did you realize?" He wiped his mouth, laid down his fork, and leaned back against the booth.

"We can't change the past. No matter how much we try. So why are we caught up in trying to fix it?" Susan cut up more of her meatloaf.

"Maybe a starting point to letting go? Karlene shoved a book at me on the flight to San Diego. Context talked about rebuilding your parental relationship."

"Then can you leave the past alone? Use the building blocks we've got and work toward building a future? One that includes us?" Susan drank more of her water.

Tim remained silent, eating as he thought. Could he do that given all that quickly happened? Did he know how to? Could Susan do the same? Was this something they could do together and separately at the same time? Answers eluded him. Frack, what a time to need his journal. Maybe the best answer was he didn't know. Susan deserved an answer. "I don't know. I just don't know."

Susan nodded, keeping her thoughts to herself since she didn't say more. Both kept eating until their plates were empty. Susan reached for the check and spoke. "I'll meet you at the car. I've got to get you home."

Chapter Twenty-Three

Four Days Later

Tim leaned back in his desk chair, his hand on the back of his head. His thoughts refused to focus on work.

Susan had dropped him off without more than a few words exchanged between them the rest of the trip. Each time he'd tried to restart the conversation from where it dropped off at the diner, she'd told him *not now*. He'd given up after the fourth time. Either she wanted him to think about what she'd asked, or he'd pissed her off. He couldn't tell which. The days that followed found him either deep in meetings or helping Karlene with unpacking—a process he hadn't planned on or enjoyed. Having her across town didn't hinder his conviction that he and Susan weren't letting this chance slip away. Most of his texts to Susan went unanswered. Her occasional short replies of "I'm fine. Thanks for asking" shed no light on where she stood on them. The auto out-of-office e-mail replies had him ready to call it quits. Then the call came. The one he wished she'd made four days sooner than later.

"Hi." Susan's voice came through the phone followed by a loud hum and crackle.

"Hi," Tim replied. He pulled his phone away from his ear, checking the volume. The indicator showed maxed out. "You sound far off."

"I'm on a boat." Susan's voice muffled. The hum's volume increased, as did the crackling. "Sorry. An old work friend contacted me last minute to help her with a renewal ceremony. I've been out of town since I dropped you off."

He'd taken three deep breaths before answering the phone. He took another, glad she was safe and talking to him. "Wish you'd let me know sooner."

"I needed space to think." Susan paused. Was she waiting for him to respond?

"And?" Tim let go a shuddered sigh, bracing for the worst.

"Breathe, please. I don't break up over the phone. Neither do you if I remember right." Susan's chuckle sent flip-flops through his stomach. Was she calling to set up a breakup date? Great, he needed that like he didn't need a hole added anywhere he didn't already have one.

"Uh-huh. Okay, I guess." Tim covered the mouthpart of his phone. He rolled his eyes skyward, silently mouthing, *Do I ask her why she's calling?*

Well, do you want to know, idiot? Great, his psyche's sarcastic wit got loose again.

Yes, I want to know.

Then ask her. I'm busy napping.

Tim snorted, wondering if others had similar-sounding consciences. Maybe his sense of humor colored his perceptions.

"What did you find out?" There. He said it. Voiced the question needling him out loud.

"I've got a lot of forgiving to do, too. I owe you an apology." Susan's voice faded, and the line went dead.

Tim sat up, trying to call her back.

"*All circuits are busy. Please try your call again.*"

He dialed again. Laying his phone down, he repeated the message he got. "All circuits busy. Please try your call again. *Fuck!*"

A cool breeze wafted across his shoulders. He looked up, catching the change in sunlight patterns dancing through the partially open venetian blinds covering his office window. Dust particles danced out of the ceiling air vent. One in particular tossed itself against the draft making its way in flight different than the others. Its destination unknown, regardless of the path it took. It continued to toss itself back into the mainstream, pushing its dance in unique patterns of its choosing. A soft chuckle drew him from his thoughts. He looked in front of him, blinking. Leslie stood just inside his office door.

"Looks like we got a similar message." Leslie pointed to the dust particles still descending through the sunbeam toward the desk and floor. "Time to stop fighting against the tide and roll with it."

"Oh," Tim said, rolling his shoulders.

"Yes. Me with the fucking state reports they want and these damn figures." Leslie tossed a file folder full of papers on top of the desk. "Come on. I'm buying lunch. We can work on these later."

Tim stood up. He picked up his phone, stowing it in his pants pocket. "Lobster truck down on the beach? I could use a walk. Mind is too full to focus on these for sure." He pointed to the file.

Leslie nodded. "I know that feeling. Let's go."

Forty minutes later, Tim sat on the bench close to the lifeguard station ten blocks from the office. He opened his bag, took out his lobster roll sandwich, and inhaled. He savored the delicious fragrance, opened his mouth to take a bite when Leslie sat down beside him.

"What's irking you?" Leslie took his similar sandwich out of his bag and bit into it. He closed his eyes and continued chewing.

Tim laid his sandwich back on its wrapping paper, leaned back, and sighed. "That obvious?"

Leslie nodded, held up one finger, and then spoke. "You were tense and palming your phone when I entered your office. I backed out. I heard you cuss through the closed door."

Tim pulled off bits of his sandwich, held it up, and replied, "Susan and I. Communication ain't going down well." He popped the food into his mouth and chewed.

"Sorry. Sometimes that happens. Nina and I been hit and miss last few days, too. Care to talk about it?" Leslie opened his bag of chips and put two into his mouth.

"Issues with where we're at and going." Tim bit into his sandwich, chewing and savoring the tangy sauce and lobster meat mixed with garlic and chipotle seasoning.

"Caught up in the past? Karlene and the girls?" Leslie stuffed some chips into his sandwich and ate it, crunching as he did.

Tim took a large swallow of his cold root beer and wiped his mouth. "Seems we're seeing more of each other from then instead of now."

Leslie chuckled. "Have you built a now to see each other in? Changed up your perceptions of each other?"

"Susan asked me about that." Tim finished his sandwich.

"What was your response?" Leslie wiped his hands, stuffed his trash in his bag, and opened his soda can.

"Said I didn't know if I could let go. I didn't have an answer for her. We didn't talk the rest of the drive home." Tim brushed his pants off, picked up his trash, and stood.

"Do you have one now?" Leslie rose and stood beside him.

"Oh, yeah. She called today. After almost nothing for days." Tim started toward the trashcan back the way they came.

"Did you get to tell her?" Leslie dropped his trash in the can, stopping next to Tim.

"No, the damn call dropped, and she's somewhere on a boat taking care of business." Tim stuffed his hands into his pants pockets and took off down the path.

Leslie caught up to him, patted his shoulder, and nodded. Neither said more as they walked back to the office. Tim glanced at Leslie twice as they waited for the light to change two blocks from their office. Crossing the street, Leslie spoke. "If you want to build a future, you need a foundation. What yours and Susan's is I can't say."

"Even my bloody horoscope says let go of things that cloud your vision. I'm beginning to think there's truth there," Tim replied.

"Sounds to me that's what you need to talk about." Leslie held the door open waiting for him to enter.

Tim entered and paused in the middle of the lobby. "There's a jumbled mess I'm sorting through. This is going to take a bit of thought and time."

"Okay, then take a few days off and sift through the pile. Put you and Susan first." Leslie looked at his watch. "I've got a meeting. I'm available if you need to talk."

Tim made his way toward the elevator as Leslie walked toward the first-floor conference room. Tim reached out to push the button. He didn't need anything from his office. He'd left his backpack at home. His days off started now. He turned around. Something about getting away urged him to pick up his pace. Outside he put on his sunglasses and didn't look back as he made his way down the street to where he parked his car.

Forty minutes later, he pulled into the beach parking lot closest to his home. His phone battery fully charged, he dialed Susan's number. It rang twice before she picked up.

"Tim, I don't have much time to talk. What's up?" She said rapidly.

Tim slumped down in his seat, cradling the phone between his chin and shoulder. "Putting me off?"

Silence followed. He licked his lips ready to speak again when Susan spoke.

"No," she began. "I'm knee-deep in business stuff. Last-minute crap that takes all my attention."

"Umm, okay," he responded. "I want to talk about what you said earlier."

"I'll call you back. The ceremony is about to start." Susan hung up before he could say yes or no.

He tossed his phone in the passenger seat, started the ignition, and backed out of the parking space. Ball was in Susan's court, and he couldn't do a damn thing except wait. Patience didn't appear to be high on his virtue list. He drove home, hoping his festering frustration cooled some before she called.

Susan gripped the boat's railing harder. She swallowed as best she could, taking a few short breaths, and looked away from the bobbing image of the beach. Nothing like getting seasick in the middle of a client's wedding. She let go of the railing, curled her lips into the best smile she could, and made her way to her observation point, a chair close to the front of the boat near the awning where the couple and minister stood.

Tim didn't deserve her curt reply. She wasn't prepared to discuss his pros and cons about repairing their past. Either they wanted a future together or they didn't. She drummed her fingers against her leg, listening to the vows the minister and couple repeated. The one part that struck her was about forgiving and letting go, moving forward and celebrating the now. How did she and Tim do that? Tim's prior response, "I don't know. I just don't know," came to mind as the recessional music began.

Susan rose, making her way toward the back of the boat. Forty minutes until they reached the wharf and the small inn where the reception would start. Forty minutes to compose her e-mail to Tim about taking the next four to five days to think about them and see to more business. Would he be willing to wait? Understand her need to let go of her tarnished view of herself and him to see what heading they were on together? She wouldn't know until they talked face-to-face, which wouldn't be until tight to Leslie and Nina's wedding. Only time and faith would get them through.

Two hours later, she had Tim's response. He waited this long to apologize and try again. Waiting a bit longer gave them both time to decide if they wanted a future together. Susan wiped a tear off her cheek. His P.S. clutched at her heart.

I want to see you again as you were in Vegas and in my bed and arms at home. Think about that until we talk in person. I hold you in my heart.

Chapter Twenty-Four

A Week Later

The music sounded like most wedding themes Tim heard before. He stood next to Leslie near the altar at the front of the church. The community chapel tucked beneath the boughs of the tall spruce trees and redwoods from the original Cascade Bay family homestead housed the two hundred guests snuggly. Beth came down the aisle first. Her dress reminded him of a starlit sky. Nice deep blue. Dottie followed Beth, wearing a matching dress. Each woman looked good. Tim smiled as Dottie reached the front pew. She reached out, took hold of her husband's hand, and let go. Beth had stopped long enough to do the same with her husband. Amongst this group of families and friends, it didn't matter. Personal touches added to the sense of joy and connection each shared with the others present.

Chords sounded as Susan entered the sanctuary. The tempo of the music changed as she started down the aisle. Tim pinched his thumb and index finger together, reminding himself to breathe. She wore her hair in a loose side braid set off by a single flower on one side of her head. Her smile lit up her face as she took a step and paused. She looked over her shoulder, turning slightly. Leslie's youngest sister's seven-year-old twins—a girl and a boy—followed Susan. Amanda's short red curls hugged her head like a glowing crown. Her crisp teal dress matched the boutonnieres every groomsman wore. Her brother, Andrew, wore a tuxedo similar to the groomsmen. Amanda walked, tossed flowers, giggled, and ran up to Susan's side. Andrew, with a sourpuss look, didn't take his eyes off the pillow he carried, holding two rings. Amanda ran back to him, calling out, "Hurry up, slowpoke. Aunt Nina has to come in, too." Amanda grabbed her brother's arm, dragging him along. He stumbled, almost dropping the pillow. He stuck his tongue out, shaking his head. He jerked his arm free and moved in front of Susan. Amanda linked her hand with Susan's and continued up the aisle in Andrew's wake.

Tim chuckled. He glanced out over the guests. Karlene sat in the middle section along with Jennifer and Hailey. Neither girl got why they had to be here. He did. Both were on probation after refusing to help Karlene unpack and set up their rooms. Next to Karlene sat Stuart Churchwell. How the two of them linked up so quickly was beside him. Karlene's sister mentioned Stuart was a cousin-in-law by a former marriage twice removed. Either way, their connection and budding whatever was their business. Tim moved up beside Leslie as Andrew reached him. Andrew handed the pillow to Leslie, saying, "I got it here, Uncle Leslie. Can I have my ball now?"

Leslie ruffled Andrew's hair and handed him the small ball. "Keep it in your pocket until the reception. Or it's back in my pocket, okay?"

Andrew eagerly nodded and joined his sister in the pews next to their grandparents. The music changed tempo and volume again. The bridal march sounded as the sanctuary doors opened. Nina entered on the arm of her father. Her smile beamed as she walked down the aisle. Nina's veil covered the top part of her head, allowing all to see and feel the warmth of her smile and joy. Tim took the pillow from Leslie, pocketing the rings. He stepped back, handing the pillow to Leslie's father.

As Leslie and Nina exchanged vows, Tim let his thoughts run back over the last week. Between work and last-minute wedding preparations, he and Susan hadn't found time to talk much. Short phone calls interspersed with texts and a few e-mails didn't quell his fears much. Even at the rehearsal dinner, she was quiet. The one thing that stood out from then was her holding hands with him whenever possible. He smiled, remembering the pleased look on her face after he kissed the back of her hand and rubbed his cheek against her knuckles. Would she agree to a trip to Vegas? Same hotel as before? Maybe even the same room...

A throat cleared, drawing Tim out of his thoughts. "The rings, please," the minister stated.

"Tim, the rings?" Leslie said, nudging him.

Tim slipped his hand into his pocket and pulled both out. "Got 'em. Here ya go."

Chortles rippled through the sanctuary. Tim smiled and nodded. Rings and their symbology followed with the final portion of the vows spoken. As Leslie turned to offer Nina his arm, he whispered to Tim, "Tell Susan soon. You two deserve a future together." He winked and started down the aisle with Amanda and Andrew following.

Tim moved up and offered Susan his arm. She took it, smiling as she did. He opened his mouth. She shook her head, saying. "Later. Not now."

His heart plummeted like a rock, sinking deep into the depths of despair. His preoccupation with failing covered more of his actions within the last week than his vision of success. How he communicated his vision remained up to him. Would he get the chance to do this soon?

The next two hours flew by. The receiving line took longer than anticipated. Photographs and flashes snapped until he couldn't make out where one started and another finished.

"Folks, can I have your attention, please?" Jeff called out. Everyone turned toward the center of the narthex where Jeff stood. "Follow me to the community center, please. Food is served."

Leslie and Nina followed Jeff and Mary first. Susan took Tim's arm, leaned closer and whispered. "We've got our own table. Couples for the wedding party tables worked. We can talk then."

"Got ya." Tim smiled as they reached the cars in the church's parking lot. He pulled his keys out of his pocket, clicked the remote unlocking the door, and let go of Susan's arm. "Your ride awaits, madam."

Opening the passenger door, he kept the door between them. Could they start a conversation on the thirty-minute ride to the community center? One that would continue as they ate? His concerns clamored for attention and position to announce their dismal prospects based on information and actions up to now.

Susan reached for the door handle after she got in. Tim shook his head. As he began closing the door, he spoke. "Let me get it, please."

Susan acquiesced, a puzzled look on her face.

Tim got in behind the wheel. He started the car glancing at Susan. She glanced at him. Backing out of the parking space, he knew he had her attention. Waiting for his clutter-filled thoughts to settle, he pondered how he would start the conversation. As he turned onto Main Street, Susan cleared her throat.

"What's going on?" she asked, her tone more subdued than before.

Tim looked at her as he came to a stoplight. "My question, too. We both have questions. Mine is why do *you* need to apologize?"

Susan turned in her seat. She waited until he gazed at her again. "Lecturing you on letting go of the past and be in the present. I wasn't doing it very well."

Tim snorted as he pulled into the intersection. "All right. How about this—neither of us had much to go on except our chemistry and past connection."

"You been talking to Nina?" Susan faced ahead.

"No. A shrink the girls and I are seeing together and individually." Tim completed his turn. He let go of the stirring wheel with one hand and held up a finger. "She had us forgive each other and ourselves out loud. It hasn't been easy, but the girls and I are talking about now more."

"Great," Susan replied. "Shall we try this?"

Tim grinned. "You bet. I forgive you for the past. I let it go."

"Good. My turn. I forgive you. I let the past go also."

"So, where do we go from here?" Tim pulled into the long line, waiting to enter the highway back into town.

"Hi. I'm not the Susan you knew then. You helped shape parts of me." Susan held out her hand.

"Pleased to meet you. I'm not that Tim you got back then either. I learned from you, too." He took hold of Susan's hand. As they inched forward in the traffic flow, he brushed his lips over her knuckles.

Susan giggled. "Well, that's a new beginning."

"Yes," Tim tossed out. "Now traffic needs my maneuvering attention."

Fifteen minutes later, he pulled into the community center's parking lot. He backed into the parking space close to the door. He unfastened his seat belt and turned to Susan. "Thanks for watching the merge spots for me. Appreciate it."

"You're welcome. What's next?" Susan opened her door.

Tim came around the car to help her out. "We get to know each other and date?'

Susan laughed. She slipped her arm through his. "Aren't we doing that already?"

Tim held a finger to his lips as they had reached the community center entrance. "Secret for further discussion."

Hours of food, toasts, and mingling passed before Tim stood next to Susan again able to say more than a few words here and there. Too many ears close by for them to talk as they had hoped. The overhead lights came up and the DJ moved to the middle of the floor. "Ladies and gentlemen, I give you Mr. and Mrs. Snider."

Leslie and Nina moved on to the dance floor. A single spotlight followed them as they danced.

Music rumbled out of the speakers close to the front of the room. Eighties dance music crescendoed into a softer, slower melody that took Tim back to junior prom. The first time he realized he wanted to spend the evening with Susan in his arms. His jealousy over her date got the better of him, and he said some of his crassest remarks that night as they left the party.

"May I have this dance?" Tim mimicked the slow dancing moves of their youth. His hands around the girl's waist, pressing close to her then pulling back as he looked down.

Giggling, Susan tried to answer him. "Y–yes. You're silly."

"With you, I'm joyous." Tim swept her into his arms and started moving out across the dance floor. Close to one darker corner, Beth and her husband swayed, holding their youngest between them. Tim nodded and twirled Susan past them. Several steps later, they inched their way into another darker corner. Dottie and her husband stuck their tongues out at them, admonishing them to find their own spot. Back across the dance floor, he spun and moved them until the music faded.

Tim nudged Susan. "There's a dark corner over there." He pointed back toward the hallway leading to the restrooms.

"Looks good to me." Susan took his hand.

Out of sight, he pulled her tight against him. He rested his forehead on hers. "You do make me joyous. Really, you do."

Susan tilted her head, lips puckered, leaning into him. He brushed his across hers. She didn't pull back. Her tongue traced his lips. She threaded her fingers through his hair, pressing her body tighter to him. There was no mistaking her interest. He opened his lips and invited her in. Hands roamed where clothing covered. Passion smoldered as hearts beat against each other. Nothing else mattered but them.

"I'd suggest getting a room, except you've shown restraint."

Tim broke off the kiss, squinting until Leslie came into view. "Jealous?"

"No. Just don't want you setting off the smoke detector." Leslie grinned, moving past him. He returned a short time later with his and Nina's jackets. "Time to toss the garter and bouquet. Then we're out of here."

"All right." Tim slipped out of Susan's arms, moving to the center of the room.

"Gents, we have a garter to help rid Nina of. Circle 'round if you are interested in catching it." Tim pulled the chair Dottie's husband held out to him into the light.

A double row of men lined up close to the chair as Nina sat down. Leslie kneeled, making a fuss about pushing her skirt up to get at the frilly lace item. He stood, pointed at Tim, and said, "You get in line, too."

Laughing, Tim joined the other men in the second line, planning to move back once Leslie made the toss.

Leslie called out. "On the count of three."

He waved the garter. "One."

Someone called out two.

On three, the men surged forward, some going behind Tim and pushing forward.

"Heads up, Tim," someone called. Tim looked up, trying to move. No luck. The garter came down rapidly toward him. He tried to duck. He couldn't due to the other men reaching up and pressing close. Maybe he could lean away. Plop, something landed on his head. He reached up. He gripped the item, knowing what it was before he brought it into sight. One blue lacy garter filled his hand. Laughter sounded. He moved through the throng, nodding as the other men congratulated him. He moved toward Susan.

"Now we have one last item to toss," Nina's voice sounded. He turned back. She stood on the chair Leslie steadied for her. "Susan, this includes you, too."

Tim watched as Susan made her way to the group of women gathering at the edge of the spotlight ring on the floor. Nina counted down like Leslie had and tossed. Tim could see Susan moving opposite many of the women and looking behind her as she did.

"Dang, missed it," one eager woman called out.

Two others missed it.

"Susan," Beth called out. "Looks like it's yours."

Susan looked up. Like with Tim, the item came at her like it was meant for her. She reached up, cupping her hands like Tim had taught her in junior high to catch baseballs in her glove. The bouquet found her. She held it up, bowed, and moved back.

Tim slipped his arms around her waist as she touched him. He kissed her neck.

Susan arched her neck, speaking as she did. "You are a joyous part of my life, too. I love you."

Music started signaling Nina and Leslie's departure. Tim took Susan's hand, moving them to one side of the arch forming. He lifted her hand to his lips and said, "I love you. Here's to a joyous future together."

Susan smiled, nodding, and replied, "Yes. Reunited by mutual choice."

Epilogue

Eighteen Months Later

Tim leaned forward, his forearms on his knees. His hands, folded together with his fingers entwined, lay between his spread legs. He looked up at the sign etched into the door glass pane. Even backward, he could make the words out as plainly as he had when he entered them four hours ago. Maternity ward said it all. Leslie sat across from him, texting on his cell phone and glancing at his watch every two to three minutes. It seemed like more. Who knew they'd share this part of their lives as succinctly as others since Leslie and Nina married. Eighteen months since Susan and he agreed upon their mutual foundation and began envisioning what building their future looked like. It hadn't been easy. Ups and downs mixed with joy and laughter. Jennifer and Hailey called him weekly. He spent dedicated time with them. Susan's insistence on this won her a partial reprieve from the girls. They no longer avoided speaking to her when they stayed with him. A lot of good stuff was happening since he and Susan married. Tim looked to where Leslie sat across from him.

"You've done this before. Do babies always take this long?" Leslie stood, glancing at his watch again. He turned and started pacing like he had twenty minutes earlier.

"They come on their time schedule." Tim chuckled. "I didn't expect to see you here. Nina's pregnancy is six to eight weeks behind Susan's."

"Nina looked at me and said now while driving home from visiting her grandmother. I didn't question her." Leslie turned back the way he came marking the aisle between sets of chairs lining the waiting room.

"Susan's water broke in the middle of cooking dinner. Thankfully my sister took over." Tim patted the chair next to him. "Sit down. Wearing a hole in the floor doesn't make them arrive any sooner."

Leslie sat down, perching on the edge of the seat. "Twins. Who knew? They don't run in either side of Nina's or my family."

"The doctor knew. He told you at your last sonogram appointment." Tim leaned back in his chair.

"Smart mouth. What about you and Susan?" Leslie turned toward him.

"One at this point. Of course, sonograms said maybe two and the doctor ruled that out." Tim gripped the arms of his chair. "Wanting more kids comes with worries, too."

"What wor—" Leslie stopped speaking as a man in blue hospital scrubs came through the door marked employees only.

"Tim," Dr. Mathers said very emphatically. "Remember how I said sometimes testing is wrong?"

Tim stood up. "Yes. Is Susan okay?"

"She and the triplets are fine." Dr. Mather turned back toward the door he came through.

Tim looked down at his feet. The floor rose up to greet him closer than he expected. He leaned forward, hands out in front of him, blinking and shaking his head. Three! Three more blessings—products of his and Susan's love. He swallowed hard. He glanced over his shoulder. Leslie smiled, standing beside him. Leslie touched his shoulder. "Good luck. We'll play name the kids again later."

Dr. Mathers' nurse stood close by. "Mr. Smith, we've got to get you gowned. Your wife is in hard labor."

Dr. Mathers strode back to Leslie. He pointed at him. "Leslie, Dr. Sandstrom asked me to get you, too. Nina's labor is progressing rapidly. Your twins are ready to meet their momma and poppa."

Tim and Leslie followed Dr. Mathers through the door. Life brought about changes and chances. Second chances happened one chance at a time. Tim's smile grew as his vision of the future formed before him. Changes and chances were there for him and Susan, together with Nina and Leslie, to shape and embrace. His life and future looked very good.

THE END

Don't miss out!

Visit the website below and you can sign up to receive emails whenever Solara Gordon publishes a new book. There's no charge and no obligation.

https://books2read.com/r/B-A-RAUJ-FQZWB

BOOKS 2 READ

Connecting independent readers to independent writers.

Did you love *Reunited By Choice*? Then you should read *Love Reborn*[1] by Solara Gordon!

[2]

Cascade Bay

Love Reborn

Torrey Neadson wants love, connection and the white-picket fence. She blew the chance at having it with Holt, once.

Holt Addison is through with one-night stands. Problem is Torrey moved on before he could tell her.

Stranded together by a freak coastal storm, they recognize what their hearts crave and hungers demand. Has distance and time undone the strength of what they once had?

Read more at https://solaragordon.com/.

---

1. https://books2read.com/u/mYZVqG

2. https://books2read.com/u/mYZVqG

Also by Solara Gordon

Cascade Bay
Love Reborn
Reunited By Choice

Peyton Corners
Falling for You
Caught by Love's Slow Burn

Standalone
A Heart's Desire
To Love You Again
To Love You Again

Watch for more at https://solaragordon.com/.

About the Author

Solara loves and lives with her partner of 21 years in the Metro DC area. What started out as a bi-coastal romance soon settled on one coast.

A vivid imagination keeps her busy creating her next fascinating romance. She enjoys creating unique characters and watching their journeys unfold. "Love freely given multiplies and will return endlessly" is a key aspect of her stories. Add in alternative lifestyles and her love for the paranormal, and the uncommon becomes the norm in many of her stories.

Her day job in the financial services industry pays the bills while she pens her erotic tales.

Read more at https://solaragordon.com/.

www.ingramcontent.com/pod-product-compliance
Lightning Source LLC
Chambersburg PA
CBHW071437260626
47170CB00008B/2749